Exclusive

Mel Teshco

Exclusive

Chapter One

The raspy, soulful voice of Amos Drynn, the lead singer of Frankenstein's Blood, swept over Tiffany like a dark caress. But she ignored the prickling of awareness that rippled over her skin and instead showed the backdoor bouncers her VIP pass.

She smiled at security as they stepped aside to allow her past and into the converted warehouse. Chin tilted high, she ignored their lustful stares as the heels of her sharp-tipped stilettos clicked down the corridor as though she'd taken to the catwalk.

She'd acted the part of temptress and femme fatale enough times to slip into its comfortable skin, and to expect both men and women to involuntarily stare. Her smile widened. To expect men, and occasionally women, to want her badly enough to pay for the privilege.

Not that it was just about looks. She'd learned early in her profession that charisma was as much about confidence and poise, and taking genuine interest in a client. She'd also learned that sometimes the wealthiest and best looking men weren't getting their deepest needs met, sexually, or emotionally.

Despite the soundproof walls, the powerful music grew in volume as Amos belted out one more song she knew word-for-word.

I want a faithful lover
A woman I can trust
Don't need a second mother
Our passion turning to dust
It's you and me, baby
You're my one and only...

Her gut pulled with envy at the woman who'd one day be just that for Amos and more. Unlike Tiffany, whose very profession ensured such a feat was near impossible.

A sudden flurry of nerves struck deep in her belly, leaving her nauseous. There were times, like now, when her confidence suddenly deserted her, when anxiety sucked away all positive emotion. Her hand shook as she opened her black clutch and slipped her VIP pass inside. The ticket would be a keepsake she'd treasure forever.

Drawing in a deep, steadying breath, she slowed as she neared the stage doors where a couple of roadies in their standard dusty jeans and logoed t-shirts watched the wrap-up of the show from the sidelines.

They didn't glance her way. They were probably well used to women hovering around the fringes, whether it was girlfriends, lovers, or wives. Not to mention paid women like herself.

After her friend and fellow call girl, Scarlet, had left behind her professional life and moved onto a brighter than bright future, Tiffany had jumped at the job offer that had come her way. Her mouth dried. What woman wouldn't want to become Amos' latest companion? But unlike Scarlet and her other friend Brandy, not every call girl was lucky enough to have a client fall in love with them.

After a failed affair with a client who was also a married man, Tiffany knew better than most that the men she met in her line of work weren't always honorable. She sighed. If Toby hadn't been her client, she mightn't now be so cynical about every other man's intentions. Instead, she'd discovered that falling in love was a huge mistake, one she didn't ever care to repeat.

She drew in another steadying breath. She'd make the most out of this assignment, her feelings firmly disconnected, just the way her client expected.

The lead singer of Frankenstein's Blood wouldn't be impressed if he knew she was a huge fan. So she'd pretend disinterest. It was why she'd deliberately avoided the concert until it was almost over. Now that she was doing her best to put Toby behind her, she'd resume her professional role, and stay that way until she was out of the call girl business for good.

That won't be happening anytime soon. She squeezed her eyes shut, doing her best to ignore the snide voice, and once again push aside the constant gnawing ache that pressed in on her from all sides.

A little over five years ago, her father had been crushed by a truck while he'd been unloading from it with a forklift. His head and spinal injuries meant he'd needed a specially designed house and full-time care. Sending him to a nursing home wasn't even an option; it'd send her once independent dad to an early grave.

How different both their lives might be right now if her mother hadn't run off with her dad's best friend... if her mother hadn't left behind Tiffany as a twelve-year-old to be raised by the man who'd been left crushed in spirit long before the truck had done the same to his body.

Tiffany's lashes fluttered apart. She didn't need her mom. She'd gotten out of the financial mess by working as an escort, and would continue to work as one for a long as it paid the bills and she'd saved enough for a secure future.

In the meantime, if Amos wanted the public to see a sexy and beautiful woman on his arm, one without any baggage, then that was what she'd give him. She wouldn't be throwing herself at him, or fall to pieces like some rabid teenage girl. She'd repress *all* of her fangirl enthusiasm.

It shouldn't be too hard a feat, not after Toby had blackened her heart with empty promises and meaningless assurances.

Sensing the attention of the roadies, she forced a smile their way. Their stares slid back to the stage as Amos' husky tone soared into a controlled tenor, and then cut off with the conclusion of the song.

The crowd roared, clapping thunderously even as Amos thanked the Sydney crowd for their support and said goodnight.

She swallowed hard. In a matter of seconds, she'd finally meet the lead singer of Frankenstein's Blood, whose raw ballads never failed to twist her insides with yearning, and whose powerful lyrics could rocket her from misery to a rush of powerful, positive emotions.

She'd soon find out all there was to know about her rock star idol. But the cynical part of her wondered if disappointment would override any and all starstruck emotion once she got to know the real him.

Life wasn't fairytales and rainbows, no matter how much she worked at making her clients believe just that.

The lead guitarist, Jaimee Redden—J.R. to all his fans—walked through the opened stage doors. His eyes widened at seeing her, before he winked and drawled, "Hey, baby, looking for me?"

Even if she hadn't sensed his swaggering self-importance, she would have smelled the whiskey on his breath a mile away.

She resisted stepping back. "No, I'm here for Amos."

Jaimee shook his head, his long, curly hair bouncing, and his eyes hardening as he looked her over again with a curled lip. "Like he needs to pay a woman to fuck and have a good time."

She'd met people like Jaimee. Deep down, they were insecure nobodies who tried to make her feel less high-class and more cheap whore. All of them were hypocrites at best and this man was no different. It was more than obvious he took advantage of the groupies. She could well imagine his personal motto. *Why pay for the cow when I can get the milk for free*?

At least she didn't exploit her clients. Men like Amos were more than willing to exchange cash for pleasure.

She smiled sweetly. "I guess you get what you pay for."

A dark, sexy chuckle sent little shivers down her spine, and she turned as Amos stepped toward her and murmured, "Not to mention less trouble, more fun."

The lead guitarist faded from existence as she swallowed past her suddenly dry throat. Up close and personal, Amos was pure masculine sin. Tall and broad, his powerful arms could easily hold a woman up against a wall while he fucked her into submission. His skin was damp with sweat, and she stifled an urge to inhale his musky scent deep into her lungs, then lick his tattooed arms and follow wherever the ink led.

Amos paused, his tight leather pants outlining an impressive bulge. Her womb clenched. Sex with most of her clients was just part of her job description, mostly pleasurable and occasionally boring. But nothing about Amos would be dull. Everything about him was exciting and she craved to get him naked and even more gloriously sweaty.

He cocked his head to the side, his stare gleaming with approval. "You must be Tiffany."

She managed a nod and a smile, her pulse beating out of rhythm and her skills as a conversationalist scattered like dust to the wind. Amos made her feel as skittish as a newly handled filly, yet sexy in a whole new way, like she was a virgin stepping out in the form-fitting, little black dress for the very first time.

"You're happy to go to the afterparty with me, yes?" he asked, looking amused by her tongue-tied silence.

She nodded again, and then managed, "Yes, of course. I'm looking forward to it."

Hopefully it wouldn't be too out there. She'd heard what went on at some afterparties. But she couldn't back out now. Her reputation was at stake, along with the VIP Desire Agency she worked for. Besides, those afterparties were one of the reasons he paid for an escort. He wanted to keep the crazies at bay, at the same time he fostered his wild boy image.

The rest of the band members marched past, a bearded man wolf-whistling in appreciation as he all but undressed Tiffany with his eyes.

Amos cocked a brow. "Piss off, Tommy, she's mine."

She recognized Tommy, he was the talented drummer whose beats held together the rock ballads, and became the frenzied, driving pulse of the heavier rock tunes. He scraped a hand over his closely shorn hair and grinned carelessly. "You always get the cream of the crop, lucky bastard."

Amos returned the grin. "Only lucky in that I have impeccable taste."

Tommy shook his head ruefully and disappeared into a door further down the corridor, the same room the rest of the band members had entered.

Amos swept out a hand. "After you, gorgeous Tiffany. I need to shower and change at my hotel before we leave for the afterparty."

She looked up at him as they strolled down the corridor, grateful he slowed his long-legged stride to accommodate her smaller steps. "I could have met you at your hotel room?"

"Yes. But I thought you might enjoy the concert first."

She hid a wry smile. "I'm not really a fan." The lie came all too easily after she'd put her trust in Toby. Her former client and lover had damaged a part of her that she had doubts would ever heal. She'd never expose the vulnerable part of her heart ever again. Not for any man.

Amos' breath whistled through his lips. "Ouch. Shot down in flames!"

Despite her best intentions, she giggled at his mock outrage, sounding more like a silly schoolgirl than the classy woman he'd no doubt envisaged. It didn't stop him from smiling and curling an arm around her, his big, sweaty body pressed against her slender frame, and his large hand covering much of her bared skin through the backless dress.

Somehow, she didn't mind, not even a little. His touch burned through her flesh and awakened dormant nerve endings, her knees going weak. What woman wouldn't have melted into a puddle of bliss at his touch? What woman wouldn't die just a little to be underneath his warm, honed body?

The opened door revealed a VIP lounge, where at least a dozen women vied for the band members' attention. One young woman in a minidress and chunky-heeled boots had already locked lips with Jaimee, both of them seemingly oblivious to their audience.

Tiffany resisted rolling her eyes. J.R. was a jerk, plain and simple. She only wished the groupie with stars in her eyes knew better. But Tiffany was grateful at least that none of the other women saw Amos bypass the room. She wanted him all to herself and was glad she didn't have to watch him fend off a dozen screaming fans, before their hostile eyes turned her way.

Despite the fact her profession paid the bills and saved her father from rotting in an old people's home, it wasn't an easy career. Little wonder her anxieties had been triggered tonight.

She exhaled once they were safely out of range of the VIP lounge. Her next inhalation dragged in Amos' delicious, musky sweat mixed with something exotic and dark. She resisted sighing. He probably had cologne made especially for him.

When something close to a purr instead rumbled deep in her throat, she gulped down the sound and distracted herself by taking in the converted warehouse building. Even with limited theater seating and tickets at a premium price, she'd heard it was the offstage shadowy intimacy, contrasting ocher walls and eclectic prints, reminiscent of bold art deco, that helped secure many top performers.

Not that Frankenstein's Blood needed the incentive of money. They'd be rolling in it already.

The bouncers she'd seen earlier barely hid their knowing smirks as they opened the back exit doors to allow her and Amos outside. Amos then led her through the reserved parking lot, to a shiny red muscle car that screamed V8 power.

He opened her passenger door, a true gentleman, and she smiled up at him and said, "Nice car."

He grinned. “Meet Suzy, my ’69 Ford Mustang.” His sigh sounded almost forlorn. “They don’t make cars like they used to.”

The door clunked shut behind her before he folded his big body into the driver’s seat and turned the ignition. The engine roared into life before he backed the car out with practiced ease.

Once out on the street, he glanced at her, the flash of streetlights revealing the interested glint of his eyes. “So tell me about yourself.”

Clients never asked about her private life, and she wasn’t about to be an open book to the first client who showed interest. She smothered a sigh. It was bad enough Toby had learned so much about her. She shrugged and said in an offhand tone, “What can I say? I’m a call girl. I fuck rich men like you for money.”

His teeth gleamed in the gloom. “What can I say? I like your honesty.”

“No point in pretending I’m something I’m not.”

“True.” His hands curled easily around the steering wheel, his energy after his big performance clearly not diminished. “I imagine taking care of a man’s physical needs is both a risky and rewarding profession.”

She looked his way, trying not to lower her defenses. He might be a rock god, but she sensed he was also a genuinely nice guy. Then again, she’d been wrong before. “Yes.”

He indicated to turn at the T-intersection ahead. “You don’t like talking about yourself. Is that a call girl thing?”

She ignored the peculiar burning sensation in her chest when she asked, “I don’t know. Did Scarlet?”

He exhaled and then cleared his throat. “To be honest, I wouldn’t know. I never asked her anything personal.” He glanced her way. “Not once.”

She refused to allow his revelation to go to her head.

Instead, she conceded, “Call girls don’t encourage personal topics. We tend to listen, not chat about ourselves.” She looked his way. “It’s all part of our service.”

He nodded. “I get it.”

She smiled, changing the subject and adding huskily, “So let’s talk about you.”

A faint frown wrinkled his brow. “You know, you don’t need to act the call girl, not for me. I’m happy for you to be yourself.”

She blinked. If he only knew how much she really did want to know about him. “I’m genuinely interested to hear more about you, especially the person behind the singer.”

He shrugged, evidently going along with her interest. “On stage, I’m basically public property. Offstage, I’m an intensely private person, despite the spotlight. Give me country peace and quiet to the frenetic pace of the city any day.”

He stopped at a red traffic light, for a moment his attention turning wholly to her. “Other than that, there’s not all that much to tell. I sing and hope someone will be inspired in some way... or at the very least enjoy my music.”

She knew without a doubt he had a whole lot more to share, but she wasn’t in the business to push for information. He’d tell her what he wanted, and she was happy with that. After all, he wasn’t the only one keeping things private. She lived in a whole different world to the life she had as a call girl.

Still, she couldn’t help but add, “Your music influences thousands of fans. I imagine it’s a heady feeling.”

He nodded. “It is. But it’s also daunting at times. What if I write a song that negatively affects someone?” He glanced back at her. “What if I sing something that reminds someone of an incident they’d rather forget?”

She couldn't help but smile. "Sometimes being reminded about something you'd rather forget is a good thing. No matter how negative it might feel at the time."

"It sounds as though you're speaking from experience."

She'd already told him she wasn't a fan. There was no way she was going to admit to the devastation she'd experienced on hearing the one song that'd reminded her all too vividly of Toby's betrayal. A reminder she needed to have so as to never let something like it happen again.

Instead, she shrugged and said, "Maybe."

He rubbed at his brow, his voice dry. "I'll have to remember you don't talk about yourself. So let's talk about something else?"

Her taut shoulders relaxed. "Sure."

He glanced her way, his stare glinting. "I imagine affecting people so effortlessly with your looks and charisma must also be a heady feeling?"

She hid a smile. As a handsome as hell rock god, he'd understand all too well.

But she'd play along. "It can be daunting at times too. High expectations and all that."

He chuckled. "Well, you have nothing to fear from me. I have no expectations aside from enjoying looking at you while we socialize until some ungodly hour of the morning."

The car dashboard was already inching toward midnight. The hours would tick by far too quickly for her liking. Still, she couldn't help but wonder if maybe he didn't find her attractive enough to take to bed. Or maybe he wasn't attracted to the opposite sex, period. No. There was too much sexual tension between them to imagine he wasn't interested.

When Amos pulled up at a hotel that gleamed golden under its many lights, and which washed him in a glow that made him appear even more magnificent, she shivered with yearning.

Even Toby hadn't affected her with this carnal need that had her pulse hammering and her womb clenching. *No* client or lover had made her feel this intensity of need.

A valet appeared out of seemingly nowhere and opened Tiffany's door. She smiled thanks before the young man handed Amos a claim ticket in exchange for a large tip. The valet beamed approval and jumped into the car to drive it to the parking area beneath the hotel.

Amos stepped toward her and held out his arm. "Let the night begin."

Chapter Two

Tiffany rode up the elevator with Amos to the top floor of the penthouse suite. Not even a minute later she stepped through its opened doors. All of her clients were wealthy and it was nothing to see beautiful living areas with sweeping views of Sydney Harbour. Not that she noticed anyway. All her attention remained on Amos as they walked through the suite.

He stopped at an inbuilt bar that gleamed under downlights. "Help yourself to a drink."

"Thanks." She slanted him a look and asked throatily, "Is there anything you'd like?"

His stare brushed over her little black dress with its lace inserts at the bodice and waistline, before moving down to her strappy stilettos with her red-painted toenails.

When his burning stare finally settled back on her face, his smile was tellingly strained. "Thank you, but no." He stepped back. "Give me five minutes to shower and change and then we'll be out of here."

She repressed a flare of shock and managed a nod before watching him with wide eyes as he strode toward the bathroom, dragging off his shirt as he went. Her mouth dried at his broad, glistening back that revealed tattoos that were surprising to say the least, particularly the white rose and red heeled shoe.

The ink had a story to tell, one she was sure was totally irrelevant to the swirling guitar and microphone tattoos on his shoulders, and the intricate, dark tribal patterns on his upper arms. Sadness for a moment welled inside. The story was one she'd probably never uncover.

Some text underpinned the images, but he stepped into the bathroom before she had a chance to decipher the words.

She blinked, then turned away to tip some scotch into a squat, crystal glass. Taking a mouthful of the strong, amber liquid, she put the glass down with a sharp clack. She wouldn't stand for rejection and she also had a job to do. Client satisfaction was her business and she wanted very much to be the woman who gave Amos exactly that.

She drew off her heels and lacy black thong, before she dragged off her dress and draped it over the lounge. Following him into the bathroom, she paused at the doorway, her nipples springing into hard buds and her breath for a moment stolen right out of her.

Steam filled the air but she saw enough of his body to know she wanted to see more. His back was to her and his face angled up into the water. Dear lord, he could have been an athlete with his wide shoulders and trim waist, and a rounded ass that was made for grasping.

He turned slightly, and her eyes widened. His cock was long, thick, and hard, the shaft roped with veins. Damn. She'd seen plenty of gorgeous—and not so gorgeous—naked bodies, but Amos' was perfection.

She opened the steamed glass door and stepped inside the shower stall about the same time his eyes connected to hers. His light blue stare darkened, his cock twitching.

"Tiffany." He growled—or was it more a groan—before he stepped toward her, his earlier rebuffal clearly forgotten.

His big wet body enveloped her, and she gasped when he spun her around and pushed her against the tiled wall. After making no attempt to seduce her, she hadn't expected his *take no prisoners* approach. He bent his head, and his mouth slammed over hers in a kiss that didn't pretend any gentlemanly intent.

She moaned into his mouth, hungry for him, for his possession. Hungry for the man who'd been her rock in an unstable world. A singer who'd lifted her from lowest of lows to the highest of highs.

Her body might be trained for sex, but she didn't need to act on her skill. Every touch, stroke, press, and grind against him was pure animal instinct.

He groaned something unintelligible before he dragged her off the wall and into the hot water pummeling around them. One of his big hands splayed across her hip, keeping her in place, while his other hand palmed the mound of her sex.

She moaned, loud and deep, grinding against his hand, desperate for his touch. He pulled his head back, water streaming down his face, down hers, and his eyes burned into hers. "You want respite?"

It was *her* job to give him the physical release he craved, not the other way around. But right then she didn't have the will to fight the need bubbling like lava inside and needing release.

She nodded, her voice cracking. "Yes."

He parted the petals of her labia and touched her clit. She leaned into him with a sharp gasp, clinging onto his shoulders for support. Damn, without her heels, he was a giant of a man. He pressed her nub a little harder, but didn't stroke. The bastard was deliberately drawing out her needs until she was all but writhing.

"Please." She whimpered.

His eyes darkened, his cock jerking against her belly.

With a harsh exhalation, he growled. "I love it when you beg, sex kitten."

Giving her no time to answer, he thumbed her sensitized clit, massaging the swollen bundle of nerves with a skill that pushed her straight over the brink.

He slid a finger into her as the first orgasm hit. Her inner muscles contracted around him and her legs went weak, but he easily kept her balanced. When he flicked her clit again, a second orgasm hit her hard.

She shuddered against his hand, and he cupped her sex in a possessive touch, while she returned to earth with her knees weak and her body warmer than honey.

His cock strained against her belly, warm and pulsating with life, and surely bigger than any client she'd had before? She licked her lips, tasting tap water but yearning to instead sample the saltiness taste of Amos' pre-cum, yearning to feel his all his hard length and breadth inside her, filling and stretching her to the limits.

She cupped his heavy ball sack and his breath sharply hissed. When she stroked his shaft up and down, he stilled her hand and shut down the water.

"You're not getting my seed out of me that easily." He growled, before he bent and lifted her against his chest. With both of them dripping wet, he carried her out of the bathroom and across the living space, before striding into a huge bedroom.

He laid her onto a bed, the mattress depressing beneath her and a soft coverlet caressing her spine. She sighed at the softness even as her stare caressed all his glorious hardness.

She could only imagine how many female fans eyeballed him in his leather pants when he was on stage. It would be those same women who'd fantasize about having his well-endowed cock pumping into them.

Too bad ladies, tonight he's all mine.

Her belly clenched and moisture that had nothing to do with the shower slicked her pussy. Her belly fluttered and her pulse pounded. She hadn't been this needy for a man since... forever.

But then, working in the sex industry, it was all too easy to take for granted great sex. She grinned. She never failed to appreciate an orgasm, not when they were too few and far between.

Amos reached into a side table to retrieve a condom before he deftly rolled it onto his shaft. "Are you ready for me, kitten?"

He even needed to ask? She cracked out a yes, before he climbed over her. His stare blazed, but she detected something else in the depths, something both primitive and gentle. And although their kiss had been savage, when he centered himself at her core, he pushed into her slowly, his thick length filling her until pleasure merged with pain.

She stiffened and he paused, waiting for her muscles to adapt, the cords of his neck sticking out with the restraint. "Are you okay?" he asked hoarsely.

She blinked. His size had obviously been a problem to the women he'd taken to bed in the past. She snuffed out an unsettling sensation that was too close to jealousy for comfort. She was a call girl; she had no right to feel that way.

A client's love life was his business, not hers.

She spoke past her scratchy throat. "I'm good."

He assessed her for a moment before his face relaxed, and he bent and kissed her. His mouth was soft and gentle, then fierce and dominating as he began moving inside her with long, slow strokes.

She closed her eyes, forgetting to breathe, forgetting to act on the call girl tricks that got a man off. Instead, she reveled in her electrified nerve endings that built pressure within. Then he lifted her knees back, and plunged deep. Her eyes widened at the different angle and nerve endings he'd hit, and at the rush of heat that pooled in her core.

His next stroke made her gasp in shock at the sparked inferno that lit up from within and shimmered through her in a cascade of rapture. She arched back and mewled long and loud, and Amos' voice was savage with triumph when he said, "I'm going to make you come all over again."

When her orgasm faded, his strokes increased, his balls slapping hard against her flesh and his jaw gritted with single-mindedness. But, this once, she wasn't mindful of her client's needs. This once, she was swept away in the moment, surrendering to the next climax that barreled through her like a tsunami, her inner muscles clamping around his cock.

Amos released his seed with a hoarse grunt of elation. And, for the first time in her profession, Tiffany wished she could feel the warm flood of his orgasm inside her. Yearned to feel his bare cock and his cum.

"Wow, kitten." He rasped. "That was... incredible."

Her lashes fluttered as she looked up at his face and drank in his profile like he was the last man on earth. "No arguments here," she said, dazed and floating down from the high of the orgasm he'd induced.

His smile didn't reach his eyes when he brushed a strand of blonde hair away from her face and said, "I bet you say that to all your clients."

She bit back a scathing reply. Of course he'd think exactly that. She was just a sex worker, after all. She kept quiet as he gently disengaged and then disposed of his condom.

When he returned he lay beside her and drew her to face him. "That was also... unexpected," he said huskily.

She smiled at him, already forgiving him for his earlier assumption. Even her heart was doing crazy little somersaults. "But it was a really good unexpected," she murmured.

He nuzzled her throat, the shadow of his bristles scraping across her skin. "Yes. Most definitely, yes."

She stretched languidly, and said deliberately, "I bet you say that to all your call girls."

He grinned. "Actually, no. I've never once paid for intimacy."

She stiffened, disbelief coursing through her. She looked up into his serious stare. *Holy shit*. He really meant it.

She swallowed, doing her best to push back a whole mountain of delight that threatened to break free. "So what *do* you pay us for?"

"Peace of mind."

He was a rock star. She thought that'd be a privilege not a handicap. Still, it wasn't her business. Her only concern should be his happiness and wellbeing, at least physically.

She brushed her fingertips down the light ripple of his abs, and he caught her hand in his before she reached his already thickening cock. "We're already late for the afterparty."

She smiled, ignoring a pang of disappointment. If she wasn't paid to do his every whim, she wouldn't have taken no for an answer. She'd never had such great sex in all her years of working in the sex industry, and she wanted almost desperately to experience it again.

She drew her hand free. "Then I'd better get some clothes on."

She slipped out of bed, feeling his stare on her as she sashayed away from him and bent just so to scoop up her thong. She stepped into the lacy piece of nothing and pulled it up her thighs.

Her nipples hardened when she caught his burning eyes, and she asked him in a throaty voice, "Are you sure you don't want to stay in?"

And fuck the night away.

His answering smile was a lazy quirk of lips. "No, kitten. I'm just taking a moment to enjoy the scenery."

She ran her hands up and down her torso, before she cupped her breasts. "Take all the time you need."

Moving back to where he lay on the bed, she climbed over him and asked, "I can't change your mind?"

Because she really truly wanted to do just that. Not because it was part of her job description. Not even because he was every woman's fantasy. It was the explosive attraction between them that she wanted to sample again and again.

"You're too sexy for you own good." He said, clasping behind her head to bring her mouth down to his. His lips were warm and sure on hers, the tip of his tongue pushing in to taste and touch.

He pulled away first, his breathing as ragged as her own and his cock thick and hard. "If my fans weren't expecting me at this party I'd stay here with you in a heartbeat. But it's those same fans that buy my albums and give me the lifestyle I'm able to enjoy. And not to mention the rest of the band and my agent would never forgive me."

His smile became a lopsided grin that looked all kinds of dirty as he lay back and pulled on her hips to bring her forward. "I'll make the time though to give you one more orgasm."

Before she could form even one coherent thought, he'd pushed aside her scrap of lace and spread her thighs wide above his face. She quivered even before she felt the first long stroke of his tongue. By the second and third strokes she was halfway to heaven, her hips moving involuntarily to grind along his mouth while his hands on her hips helped guide her.

He moaned against her clit and she inhaled sharply, every nerve ending down there quickening and swelling. Only when his big hands stilled on her hips, stopping any movement so he could lash her clit and then suckle the flesh like she was the finest lollypop, did she comprehend the true extent of oral pleasure.

She bucked against his mouth as she detonated, moaning something incomprehensible while little aftershocks left her shuddering and trembling. He licked her passion like he was a man starving, tasting her essence before he released hold of her and she collapsed onto the bed beside him.

Holy smokes! Having one orgasm was a triumph, but three of them? It almost blew her mind.

Amos turned to her, his lips wet and glistening, his eyes fierce with need. He fisted his cock and stroked up and down, his stare glittering at her nakedness.

With a ragged sigh, he released his cock. "Fucking you will be all I think about every minute of the night until I sink into your gorgeous pussy again."

She leaned close and kissed him, and his big hands outlined her jaw as he kissed her back with a fierceness that showcased just how much he wanted her again.

Tasting her musk on his lips, she pulled back with a self-satisfied smile. “Let’s get dressed.”

Ten minutes later, Amos had dragged on dark designer jeans that were ripped at the knees, a Frankenstein’s Blood black t-shirt and a leather jacket. His casual look leant him a dangerous air that fascinated her all the more.

She tugged on her dress and, after pushing into her heels, she attempted to fix her hair. He stepped toward her and she realized his height made her even more hyperaware of him. Like his sheer size and musculature would protect her from anything bad.

She withheld a sigh. A pity her other clients rarely inspired such confidence.

He put an arm around her and winked. “Somehow you look even sexier with bedroom hair and smelling of sex.”

Her womb clenched even as her heart warmed.

She pushed aside any feelings for her client and murmured throatily, “I have you to thank for that.”

“On the contrary, I should be thanking you.” His eyes heated. “I want to taste you all over again. And I want this damn afterparty over and done with.”

Amos followed Tiffany into the back of the stretch limousine that’d waited overtime to take him to the afterparty. He nodded at the chauffeur who swept their back door closed, but Amos wasn’t overly chagrined. In fact, he was selfish enough right then not to care about his lateness.

All he cared about was the woman whose silver-blonde hair fell in disarray down her back and framed her incredible body. Not to mention her gorgeous, heart-shaped face. He couldn't stop staring at his escort for the night. Damn, when had being with a paid woman made his cock jerk to attention and his heart do a slow somersault in his chest all at the same time?

Of course all the call girls he'd hired had been beautiful, that was a given. But none had affected him like Tiffany. None had shot down the womanizing J.R. with such ease, nor made him catch Amos breath on first sight and want to take advantage of the fact he'd paid for more than just social chatter.

He'd already had a raging hard-on at leaving Tiffany in his penthouse while he'd washed away his sweat from the concert. All he'd wanted was to get even sweatier with her beneath him, moaning his name.

When she'd stepped into the shower with him, all tangible shred of self-control had evaporated as surely as the steam sucked into the overhead exhaust fan. He hadn't cared about how many men she'd serviced before him. All he'd cared about was how much he wanted to sink into her sweet pussy and suck her delectable breasts.

Bloody hell. If he wasn't careful he'd be keeping Tiffany, or whatever the hell her nonworking name was, around far longer than appropriate. Except he wouldn't let that become a reality, not when Jasmine noted his every move and every reaction to other women.

He shifted uncomfortably on his seat, as much from the damn erection in his pants as it was for the guilt that pulled at him every which way for putting any woman at risk.

Jasmine was mentally unstable. It was the biggest reason he never dated a woman more than a handful of times. It was also a reason he now avoided groupies at all cost. Jasmine had been one of those beautiful groupies he'd spent some time with after a concert, wining and dining her before taking her home to bed. She'd imagined that one time meant they were committed to one another. She still imagined she'd caught him in her sticky web and trapped him for good.

Not. A. Chance.

He was only glad he always used protection, because he'd bet everything he had that she would have played the pregnancy card real fast.

He dragged his stare away from the gorgeous silver-haired siren next to him and stared out the tinted window. He loved his freedom. Loved having no other responsibility in his life other than writing songs and singing to his fans. As for children... they were a long way down his list of future accomplishments.

Yet, even with that knowledge, he was drawn to Tiffany, wanted almost desperately to get to know her fully. She was a woman with many layers, and he wanted to delve deep and uncover her every gorgeous facet.

"Are you okay?"

Tiffany's soft, husky voice dragged him from the whirlpool of introspections and made him realize how easily she'd read him. His heart warmed and a foolish part of him also yearned to have her know him more than skin-deep.

He pushed aside the silly fantasy. "Yeah, sorry. I'm all good."

The fantasy of having Tiffany in his bed was more than enough.

She smiled and put a hand on his jeans-clad leg. He almost groaned at her touch, which seemingly scorched him through the denim and onto his skin, a burn that travelled like quicksilver straight to his dick.

"You looked like you were a hundred miles away." Her beautiful, icy blue eyes reminded him of the glow that was generated from a blue flame. "Is it a woman?"

He sucked in a breath. Did her clients often fuck her in their bedroom then gaze wistfully into the distance thinking of some other woman... a girlfriend, maybe even a wife? He grimaced.

He didn't belong in that category, no matter what Jasmine's twisted mind told her. "No. I don't have another woman waiting for me at home."

Tiffany's pearly white teeth gleamed in the intermittent street lights. "I'm glad."

He smiled in return, his chest tight with unfamiliar emotion. "So am I."

Otherwise, I'd never have met you.

Chapter Three

Tiffany tried not to read into anything Amos had said. After all, he was nothing more than her client who'd paid big money to take her into his bed.

Except, if what he said was true, he'd never paid for sex before, and presently didn't have a relationship with another woman.

Despite herself, she was flattered and more than a little bit thrilled. She was used to being admired, but that her rock idol also seemed to genuinely like her was more than she'd ever expected. That he was also a genuinely decent man was just a bonus.

The limousine climbed to the top of a summit, where big houses with their big windows took advantage of Point Piper's views, before the driver stopped in front of a sprawling, white mansion. She swallowed back another surge of anxiety. Sex with strangers she could do, but socializing with a crowd of Amos' avid fans... it was intimidating to say the least.

The chauffeur opened their passenger door, and then Amos led her to the grand entrance of big double doors.

"Are you ready for this?" he asked, as though sensing her trepidation.

She nodded, forcing back control. "Ready as I'll ever be."

A doorman pulled open the front door. She managed a smile and dragged in a steadying breath as easily a hundred people, milling in the huge room in front of them, stopped their chatter and turned to see the guest of honor in the doorway. The chatter then became a faint roar.

Wrapping a protective arm around her, Amos stepped into the melee. But as he stopped and spoke to the different people he knew, introducing her to everyone as his 'date,' she was made to feel more comfortable that she imagined possible.

And, although she knew it was an act, when he flashed a knowing grin, or squeezed her shoulders in reassurance, she was sucked in by his charm and charisma, made warm by his attention.

"Enjoying yourself?" he asked when they walked away from yet another lot of fans and had a moment to themselves.

She smiled up at him, and he brushed his thumb over her lip before she answered. "I'm enjoying seeing how much your fans love you."

A waiter with a tray of champagne flutes headed their way, and Amos passed her a glass before he secured one for himself. She took a deep swallow of the bubbles, and Amos leaned down to kiss the moisture from her lips.

"It tastes better off your lips than from a glass," he murmured.

She giggled, already feeling lightheaded and as if she'd drunk more than one sip. "You're good for my ego."

His eyes glowed. "Believe me, I don't say anything I don't mean."

Her throat dried at his intensity. Before she could think of a vaguely sophisticated reply, a suave, thirty-something man broke free from a group of suited, executive types. "Amos."

Amos nodded. "Stephen."

The other man arched a blond brow. "I'm glad you decided to show up."

Amos shrugged. "I must admit I considered forgoing the evening. But I've never let my fans down, and I don't intend starting now."

Stephen glanced her way, his stare cool and more than a little dismissive, before he focused once again on Amos. "True, but you were late... and now appear more preoccupied than usual with your... friend."

Tiffany hid a frown. Why did men like Stephan have a problem with her being a call girl? Amos was single and rich, and was fortunate enough to be able to spend his money however he liked.

Amos' expression darkened, but he kept his tone even when he said, "What man wouldn't be preoccupied in the company of this gorgeous woman?"

Stephen nodded sagely. "True." He swept a hand toward the end of the room, which looked more like a huge foyer of some grand hotel. "We've set up a signing table over there. The rest of the band is waiting for you."

Amos nodded, though going by the tension settling across his face, he was reluctant to leave her. "I'd better get to it then." He turned to her, his stare assessing. "Tiffany, I'll leave you in the care of my manager."

She nodded and forced a smile. "I'll be fine. Enjoy yourself."

He bent and pressed another kiss to her lips. "It shouldn't take too long."

She nodded, watching as he then moved through the crowd.

"You're a lucky woman."

She turned back to Amos' manager. "Yes, I am."

Stephen nodded. "I am too. I've been managing Amos and Frankenstein's Blood since the start, a little over five years now."

"Really?" The jerk made it sound as if *he* was the one who'd made them famous.

His eyes hardened. "Just remember you'll only get a night with him. You'd better enjoy him while you can."

A shiver of unease trickled down her spine. Was that a warning? A message for her to stay clear of Amos after their one night together? She brushed aside the doubts.

She was letting her damned anxieties get to her. "I fully intend to."

"Good." He looked appeased. "Fucking a stranger is one thing, but having a girlfriend holding him down and distracting him on tour is quite another."

Her lip curled. "Seems it's not his best interests you're worried about, but your own."

Draining the last of her drink, she turned, and accepted another champagne flute before she wandered away from the obnoxious man and through the crowd. Many of the fans, male and female, wore the black Frankenstein's Blood t-shirt Amos wore. Except he'd looked perfect in it, while everyone else looked washed out.

Amos had a certain swagger, a cool vibe that was as charismatic as his gorgeous looks. Not to mention the fact he could sing the pants off any song.

Not that she was biased or anything.

She tossed back a mouthful of the champagne, letting the bubbles warm her veins and loosen the tension across her shoulders.

An older man in a suit squeezed past her in the throng, his hand moving to rest on her collarbone and his eyes lingering approval at what he saw. She hid a frown and pushed past him, not giving him a chance to make a move.

She knew the type. Mature enough to know his way around a woman's body, good-looking enough to get most of those women he wanted into his bedroom. But mostly, successful enough to draw attention from the few women who wouldn't otherwise have been interested.

You still couldn't afford me.

Besides which, Amos was the only man—client—she needed to impress. Draining the last of her champagne, she handed it to an obliging waiter who offered her a full flute in return. She declined. She was a professional worker not a guest. She wouldn't let her reputation or that of her agency down by drinking herself into a blathering mess.

She stood back and watched the crowded signing table. Amos smiled and spoke to his fans at the appropriate moments, and yet she couldn't fail to notice he looked distracted. He autographed a CD case and looked up, his eyes meeting hers. Her breath rushed out even as her insides melted. She dragged her stare away. She had to distance herself from him, had to ensure she kept things strictly professional.

He paid her bills, nothing more. The pleasure he'd also given her was just an unexpected windfall.

Someone put on the loud music of Frankenstein's Blood. Her tension eased and she swayed to the beat and smiled. The afterparty wasn't half bad after all. Her favorite band never failed to put her in a great mood. A few more people danced, and soon half the mezzanine floor was filled with people dancing and grinding.

"Hey."

She swung around to view a young man—late twenties at best—with his formal dark jacket, red silk shirt, and dark slacks.

His teeth gleamed white in the darkened room, and he had to all but shout when he asked, "You're here with Amos, right?"

She nodded. "Yes."

He leaned close, his body inches from hers and his mouth close to her ear when he sighed theatrically and announced, "I should have known. He has flawless taste in women." He looked down at her, his eyes glinting. "But they never last long."

She bit back a laugh and brushed aside lingering envy for the woman who'd one day snare Amos. Was this yet another man giving her a warning?

"I won't hold that against him."

For obvious reasons.

The man's grin widened, his approval all too clear. "He'd be crazy to move on from you. But, if he does, I'd love to meet up with you sometime." Before she had the time to refute the idea, he added, "My name's Harry Madossa. I own the chain of Heavy-Weight fitness centers across Australia and New Zealand."

She nodded. She knew the place. It was one of the gyms where Brandy and Scarlet had often worked out.

He leaned closer but still had to shout, "I can afford you. But only if you're interested."

Somehow, his gentlemanly need for her approval before he became her client left her feeling a little sick inside. Exposed. He'd obviously used the VIP Desire Agency services in the past and had seen the portfolio of photos of each woman. "You'll have to contact the agency and talk to Maisey."

He nodded. "Will do."

His stare jerked to someone behind her and he swung away with a brief smile and wave. She turned to face Amos, her belly sinking. This was *not* what she wanted her client to hear.

"Soliciting on our date, Tiffany?" he asked.

Before she could find a suitable response, he took her in his arms. A hand on her ass pushed her against the thick wedge of his groin, his other hand splaying behind her shoulders as he gritted out, "You're not dating anyone but me for the foreseeable future."

She gulped at his expression, at his stiff posture, glittering eyes, and his locked jaw that screamed possessiveness. What'd brought this on all of a sudden?

She tilted her head back. "You don't get to have any say on my client list."

His eyes darkened and her breath quickened. God, what was it about this man that made her want to please him, to acquiesce. Maybe it was because she'd yet to see this side of him, yet to fully witness the strength of his emotions.

"We'll see about that, kitten."

The song ended and a rock ballad took over, one of her favorite Frankenstein's Blood songs. He swung her around, an adept dancer who had her automatically following his lead. Her breasts hardened as he looked down at her with more intensity than any client had the right to show.

She blinked. "Why do you care so much, you hardly know me?"

A flashbulb lit up the room and his face darkened at the media intrusion, even as he rasped, "We'll discuss this at the hotel."

"You've finished the signing?" she asked, voice breathless at the thought of once again being underneath his hard, gorgeous body.

"Right now, I don't much care about the damn signing."

"Your fans—"

"Can suck it up." His eyes blazed with intensity. "Let's get out of here."

"After I use the ladies' room." She managed a smile. She needed a second to collect herself and get her nerves under control.

He nodded sharply. "I'll be waiting, don't take long."

She felt his eyes on her the whole way and, once inside the ladies', was torn between relief at having a wall between them, and a need to have his all-consuming gaze on her once again. She splashed some cool water on her wrists, her anxiety dimming.

Where had the gentleman singer gone she'd met just a few hours earlier? She'd had a few scenarios of clients whose lust was all-consuming, but never on a first date. And never by someone who could have just about any woman he wanted.

She dried her hands and looked into the mirror. She couldn't deny she'd been blessed with stunning good looks, enhanced by expertly applied kohl to her eyes and shiny, cherry-red gloss to her lips. But there were plenty of beautiful women in the world. It wasn't enough of a reason for Amos to want her with such... ferocity.

She shivered at the images flashing across her mind at their recent lovemaking. Amos was all alpha male and hot as sin. She'd pinch herself if it wasn't for the fact their relationship was strictly professional.

Yeah, don't ever forget that. Amos isn't interested in you on a personal level. He wants to sate his lust, nothing more.

She finger-combed her hair. It really *was* bedroom tousled. Amos' fans would know the reason behind his late appearance. She blew out a slow breath. At least he'd upheld his bad boy image. The women would probably go even crazier over him.

She uncapped her lip gloss from her clutch purse and leaned forward to reapply it as two other women clattered into the ladies' room, their voices loud and slurred.

"Amos is so friggin' hot, I almost creamed my panties when he looked my way."

"Oh, please, everyone knows he was craning his neck to look for that blonde piece of fluff he came here with."

Tiffany recapped the lip gloss as the women went into the stalls side by side, neither one of them noticing her. They were too busy with their rabid gossip.

"Who could blame him, that woman is frigging gorgeous."

"According to J.R., she's a hooker, clearly not girlfriend material." The other woman giggled. "Besides, why the hell would Amos need to pay for a fuck when we'd do him for free?"

"He could have us both at the same time."

As the women snorted at their own joke, Tiffany fled from the ladies' room back into the crowd, her heart sinking to her toes and her belly tight with despair. Why did other women with their normal lives always make her feel so unclean? She grabbed a drink and gulped it down, careless of the hit of alcohol. She wanted only to wash away the flurry of panic once again filling her from the inside out.

How many other people in the room knew she was Amos' escort? Bad enough the grapevine meant she'd put up with intense dislike from any number of other women at the afterparty, but to have the men openly ogle her as though she was a piece of meat at the markets... suddenly she hated this feeling of being public property.

But that's what you are. Men buy your body. And women are threatened by you.

She met Amos' eyes from across the room where he waited, some suited guy taking advantage of his being alone to yammer into his ear. She sucked in an unsteady breath. Her heart beat like a drum in her ears. She couldn't face Amos, not now, maybe not ever. The whispers had probably already reached his ears, made him ashamed to be with her.

She swung away, but not before seeing his eyes widen, as though aware of her intent. She didn't wait around to see his reaction; she was too busy escaping from him... from the crowd.

Once outside, she ran toward a man who was about to get into his Ferrari. "Wait!" she called out, her voice shrill.

He turned and she saw that it was Harry, the one and same man who'd taken a liking to her earlier. He smiled, looking genuinely happy to see her. "Changed your mind?"

She swallowed back the lump in her throat, trying not to notice how raw and exposed her nerves felt, how sensitive to the negative emotions that crawled through her. "I... I just need a lift."

"To?

"Anywhere but here."

"I see." He opened the passenger door and she climbed inside. "Then, by all means, be my guest."

"Tiffany, wait!" Amos shouted.

Harry grinned and pushed the door shut and she was enveloped in leather and quiet. As Harry climbed into the driver's seat and started up his car with a roar, she turned to see Amos put his cell phone to his ear, his face taut and his eyes on the car with its tinted windows that hid her.

Harry pulled the car away from the curb, sending her a quizzical look. "What happened back there? Is everything okay?"

She looked out the windshield. In her profession, it didn't pay to develop feelings for a client. It was even worse when the client wanted more than good, old-fashioned sex. "I realized Amos can't be my client."

The other man whistled. "That's too bad... for him." He put a hand on her thigh. "But good for me."

She pulled free of his touch. The last thing she wanted was another man's proprietary hands on her. He might be good-looking and rich to boot but, right now, she wanted nothing to do with him. Not when Amos was first and foremost on her mind.

A supermarket appeared at the end of the block. "Would you mind please dropping me off here?"

His brow creased as he slid an appreciative glance over her. "You're hardly going to buy milk looking like that."

But he did as she asked anyway. As he pulled into the car park, he handed her his business card and said huskily, "I'll look forward to seeing you soon."

She tucked the card into her purse and climbed out of his car, then watched as he pulled back out into the traffic. Had he already booked her in at the agency? Her belly pitched sickly. She had a feeling he'd pull out all stops and work fast to get what he wanted.

Retrieving her cell from her clutch bag, she put a call straight to the agency for pickup. Except when Amos' limousine pulled into the car park beside her, she disconnected the call before Maisey answered, and turned to face the man who made her anxious for all the wrong reasons.

Amos stepped out of the long car, his eyes snaring hers. "Tiffany, what the hell? Why did you run? What made you so damn scared?"

Where did she start? The slow simmer of anxiety had been building over the last seven years, exacerbated by a feeling of separation from everyone else. It was as if she was now ceding to her impotence, of never being good enough for anyone but her clients, and not quite keeping her head above water. Then there was Toby's rejection and her attraction toward Amos. Little wonder she'd surrendered to a full-blown panic attack.

She swallowed. "I was... drowning," she admitted in a small voice.

He swore under his breath, but not because he was angry at her weakness, she knew right away he was grateful for her honesty, for not trying to run away again from the crux of the problem.

"Come here," he ordered brusquely, sounding less like a rock god and far more like a sensitive soul who was drawn to her frailties.

She stepped into his arms with a sigh of capitulation, reveling in his strength and his warmth, his compassionate understanding. "I'm sorry for running," she murmured against his chest.

"Not as sorry as I am."

She looked up at him with a wobbly smile. "Not the greatest call girl, am I?" If she'd been with any other client, she might well have lost her outstanding reputation along with her agency's.

"Thank god for that," he murmured, then cupped under her chin and added, "Because you're the sexiest damn call girl I've ever laid eyes on... and I've seen more than my share."

Her smile widened, her heart melting at his words. Maybe if he'd slept with all those escorts she would've felt differently. But he hadn't and, despite her best intentions, she felt... special. Privileged. "Thank you."

He bent his head and kissed her, partaking of her mouth like she was the finest wine. His lips were gentle and warm, his tongue grazing hers, the act intimate and persuasive, not unlike his music.

When he finally drew back, she wasn't unaware of his thick arousal pressing against her, of the glint of need in his stare. "Let's go back to my room," he said huskily.

Chapter Four

She nodded, her belly quivering and her breasts hardening with anticipation. Forget that she was his escort who was paid to pleasure him. This once, she wanted to be with him like she'd never wanted to be with another client ever before. She wanted to make it good for him, to ensure he never forgot their time together.

Twenty minutes later they stepped into the hotel's elevator. She was aware of his eyes never once leaving her as they ascended to his penthouse suite, the heat in the air between them shimmered like a hot summer's day.

She'd never once experienced this heightened sense of awareness, this electrified frisson of need firing through her body and activating every single one of her nerve endings. She'd grown jaded of the sex game; looked at her clients through world-weary glasses until the sex itself had even dulled.

It'd taken Amos to jolt her senses awake, Amos to make her feel alive again.

The elevator doors opened and the automated downlights flicked on as he took hold of her hand and led her through the open living room and into his bedroom.

He turned her to him at the foot of the bed, his free hand brushing some of her hair from her face. "You're the most beautiful woman I've ever seen," he murmured throatily. "And I want you in my bed again tonight. I want to wake up beside you."

Her legs weakened, and she realized he hadn't touched her intimately yet, but already her thong was moist. If she didn't know better, she'd truly believe he had feelings for her... strong feelings. But she'd never been a believer in love at first sight. He'd never met her before today and though she'd had a crush on him because of her love of his music, it hardly counted on a personal level.

Except the intensity of his expression almost had her believing the way he acted with her wasn't normal behavior. And though it was her job to please him, it was her heart that had her say, "I want that too," while bricking a wall around that part of her that wished it wasn't just for this night.

Relationships weren't part of her lifestyle, not with her career, and certainly not with her personal life. When survival was all she knew, she'd had little choice but to embrace the sex industry.

His hands moved to clasp behind her head before he kissed her, his lips already so familiar even as his touch sparked thrilling desire within. She groaned into his mouth, but she couldn't move, not with him holding her in place. Her lungs filled with his breath. Her lips tingled at his alpha control. At the way he took charge and let her relax and not second-guess her client's every need.

When he lowered her onto the bed, she was a willing participant... more than willing. She was feverish for him.

She toed of her heels before he peeled off her dress and panties. Then he thrust off his leather jacket before she helped him drag off his t-shirt and jeans, followed by his boxer briefs.

She was left panting and hot as he took the handful of seconds needed to slide on a condom. Then she was lost underneath him as his weight pinned her to the bed and his mouth pinned her head to a pillow. She writhed at his pulsating length, lying against her belly, and he groaned before moving down a little, getting into position before he pushed into her and they were as one.

His growl merged with her hissed breath. And then he was thrusting and she rhythmically moved beneath, counterthrusting until the friction of their flesh burned and their breaths and groans were in unison as they kissed. When they finally pulled apart, his mouth latched onto her breast. She gasped, arching her back as he suckled and laved her sensitized nipple before giving her other breast the same treatment.

Her whole body tingled by the time he kissed his way back up her neck, lingering on her pulse point, and then catching her mouth with his once again. And all the while he pushed in and out of her, his pace quickening as their urgency built and their need for release burgeoned.

Her hands curled around his smooth, big shoulders as tremors of sensations rippled through her, making her writhe. When an orgasm then ripped through her body, she arched her neck, crying out something unintelligible. All she knew for sure was that nothing had ever felt this good. No one had ever given her this much pleasure.

Amos thrust deep and then exhaled sharply as he too succumbed to orgasm, the cords of his neck jutting out and his eyes glittering brightly. He groaned and then folded over her, pressing kisses to her throat, her jaw, before taking over her mouth.

"Mm," he murmured against her lips. "I don't think I'll ever get enough of this with you."

Her breath shuddered as Amos slipped out of her, disposed of his condom, and moved back to take her in his arms.

"Thank you," he murmured.

"For?"

"For staying the night here with me."

"It's what you pay me for," she said sleepily.

She didn't have time to think on the stiffening of his arms… his whole body. She was warm and cocooned by his strength, and bliss was stealing through her, thanks to the aftereffects of orgasm.

Her eyes fluttered closed and she was drifting to sleep when she felt the press of his lips on her scalp. Sleep was dragging her under when she heard Amos' crooning voice, singing her to sleep.

She was too far gone to catch the words.

Tiffany woke to Amos' arm slung across her torso. She wiggled out of his hold before she climbed out of bed to the weak rays of sunlight filtering through the tinted windows. She blinked before she took a moment to drink in the man sprawled under the covers, fast sleep.

In repose he was a study of masculine gorgeousness. Even the stubble on his jaw looked perfect against the snowy white sheets and his tanned physique. His ink somehow only added to the overall effect. She just wished he'd lay on his belly so she could take a better look at the images and writing she'd glimpsed when he stepped into the bathroom.

She twisted away. It was better that she didn't know. Better that she kept her distance and gathered her shattered defenses around her. Amos made her feel vulnerable. Perhaps it was because it was so soon after thinking herself in love with Toby.

Thinking herself in love? Her breath hitched. Why was being with Amos making her doubt her feelings for Toby? Like whatever she'd felt had been an empty shell of what real love could be with someone like... this man.

Repressing a sigh, she pulled on her dress and lacy thong, scooped up her clutch bag and shoes before she walked barefooted out onto the balcony. Retrieving her cellphone she put a call through to the agency for pickup.

Finishing the call, she dropped her purse, shoes, and phone onto a little, round, glass-topped table and curled her hands around the balcony railing, staring mindlessly at the views of the water and early risers.

Cars crawled past in already congested lanes, while fitness fanatics jogged or walked below on the sidewalk. A spandex-clad couple powerwalked with a black Labrador straining on its leash.

Everything seemed so normal, yet all she could think about was the man in the room she didn't want to leave... and another new client tonight she didn't want to fuck.

But then in a perfect world Amos would be her one and only lover. In a perfect life, her father wouldn't be disabled and hurting. In a perfect reality, she'd be having sex with Amos for the pure joy of it, without the exchange of cash. But such a dream was impossible. She had bills to pay.

She heard a soft tread behind her before his hands slid around her waist. "Good morning, kitten."

She shivered at his warm breath on her scalp and the way his hands seemed to belong around her. "Morning," she said huskily.

He drew her around in his arms and she tilted her head back to face him. She'd never felt so small... so vulnerable. She pushed away any and all emotion and focused on the man causing them.

He was wide awake; sleep had seemingly fallen off him. His eyes searched hers, as though seeking answers he didn't want to vocalize. "Tell me you weren't leaving without saying goodbye."

She blinked. "Our time is up."

His stare darkened. "Is that all I am to you, an hourly rate?"

She swallowed back a sudden yearning to be anything *but* his paid fuck. "That's all you can ever be to me."

His jaw tightened. "We could be so much more than that."

"No, we can't." She didn't look away. "Tell me you could bear to be with a lover whose life revolves around other men, a lover constantly distracted by thoughts of her next client."

He flinched. "Were you thinking of another man just now?"

"It doesn't matter—"

"It does."

She swallowed. If only Amos knew how little she wanted to be with another client. If only he knew how much she wanted to simply stay here instead.

Thank god, he knew none of her thoughts. Had nothing to use against her.

His lips thinned. "So you're seeing another man tonight?"

"Yes."

"Where?"

She stiffened, and said flatly, "That's none of your business."

His grip firmed, his nostrils flaring. "I'm making it mine."

Amos was a protector not an abuser. Even when he all but vibrated with tension, she trusted in his rationale. He wanted her, but he wouldn't force her to do his bidding. Her belly twisted, but not in fear. No, it was excitement that left her buzzing and exhilarated. If Amos set his sights on her, an intrinsic part of her just knew he'd do whatever needed to attain her.

She stepped out of his arms and he released her, if somewhat reluctantly. She sighed. It surely wouldn't hurt to relent a little when he'd shared so much.

"My client has a room booked at the Park Hyatt." She managed a smile, though she felt the sadness leaking through. "Not every man wants to show me off outside the bedroom."

He didn't say a word, but she felt his eyes on her when she stepped toward the glass table and retrieved her clutch purse. Pushing her feet back into the stilettos, she turned to him one last time to say goodbye. He strode to her and crushed her to him, pouring his mouth and body over hers as though stamping her to him so she'd never forget him.

God, his lips were soft velvet even as his skilled mouth was firm and unyielding. His broad shoulders bunched under her hands and she clung onto him like a limpet who wanted so much more than his kisses alone. She drew in a shaky breath when he finally pulled away.

Didn't he realize he was unforgettable?

His face blazed with passion even as it was set with reserve. "I'll see you again... soon."

If she'd had anything to say, no words could be scraped from her thick throat. Instead, she nodded and whirled away, escaping through his penthouse suite and out to the elevator.

It wasn't until the doors slid shut and the elevator started its downward propulsion that she could properly breathe again. Could finally drag back her wayward emotions and lock them away where they belonged.

She needed, desperately, for some distance from Amos. She dragged out her cell phone with shaky hands. She needed some advice, which meant meeting up with her two best friends from the VIP Desire Agency as soon as humanly possible. Maybe then she could gain some perspective and untangle the chaos of her emotions.

She only hoped Eloise and Anna had the answers she needed.

"Natalie, please tell me you're not still mooning over Toby?"

For a moment Natalie forgot she was no longer Tiffany, the call girl. For a moment she even forgot Toby had been the man she'd badly wanted in her life.

She forced a smile and turned to Eloise, focusing on the exotic, dark eyes staring back at her. Little wonder so many men asked for Eloise, or Savannah as she was known in the VIP Desire Agency. She was stunning.

"To be honest, I was thinking about last night."

Eloise's eyes widened. "Ooh. Don't leave us in suspense. What happened? Was the client anyone we know?"

Natalie looked at her other friend, Anna, or Candy as her clients knew her, even as she suddenly wished that Kate and Claire were still a part of her VIP circle of friends. Kate and Claire—Brandy and Scarlet—had not only fallen in love with one of their clients, they'd married them too, and were in the process of living their own happily ever afters.

Not that she begrudged the two gorgeous women finding their soul mates. She just... yearned for their advice. She wouldn't dare yearn for what they had now, it was beyond her reach. And wishful thinking wouldn't bring her anything but heartbreak.

Anna arched a brow, her hazel eyes alight with amusement. "You can tell us anything. Our lips are sealed, we promise."

Natalie smiled. The beautiful Anna had stepped admirably into Kate and Claire's shoes. And now it was Anna, Eloise, and herself who shopped, dined, and laughed together and occasionally drank too much at bars. They were a trio who turned heads wherever they went, even when not dressed in their sexy escort outfits.

Natalie brushed a hand over her blonde hair she'd pulled back into a severe bun—it matched her mood—before she flicked restless hands over her black pantsuit with its chunky, silver choker neckline.

She sighed. "I know I can trust you girls." They leaned in and she said, "I was with Amos Drynn last night."

Eloise jumped up and squealed. "*The* Amos Drynn? Frankenstein's Blood, Amos Drynn?"

Natalie giggled, despite her churning emotions. "Yes and yes."

Eloise's eyes widened even more. "Was he sexy and dangerous like his pictures?"

Anna sighed. "I'm thinking he's charming and gorgeous like his rock ballads."

Natalie pushed her garden salad away. She didn't want diet-conscious food for lunch, not right then. She wanted a meat pie and chunky fries slathered in gravy. She wanted a tub of hokey pokey ice-cream. But mostly she wanted Amos, naked and in her bed.

Not that she'd ever brought a client home. No. Way. That was inexcusable and reprehensible... if only she could chase the thought out of her head.

"Well?" Eloise demanded.

"He's sexy and dangerous, but he's also charming and gorgeous." She grinned at her friends' palpable excitement. "And did I mention he's a little bit of an alpha in bed?"

Eloise clapped a hand on the table, making her wine glass and cutlery rattle. "Holy shit, Natalie! Dare I ask if this means you've gotten over Toby?"

Natalie's smile slipped. "To be honest, I don't know. When I was with Amos, it was as if no other man existed."

Anna put a hand over hers and asked gently, "And now?"

Natalie exhaled softly. "And now I'm too scared to trust my instincts." Thanks to Toby, she'd learned firsthand her instincts sucked. She looked at each of her friends. "Honestly though... enough about me. What about you two, what is going on with your love lives?"

Eloise's expression shifted into a faraway look. "I can say without a doubt it would be all too easy to fall in love with the Wolfe brothers."

"But?" Natalie asked.

"But they've been getting... possessive lately."

Anna sighed. "Is that a bad thing? They like you a lot, yes?"

Eloise nodded. "Yeah, I guess they do. Or maybe it's more that they don't want to share me with anyone else."

Natalie frowned. In her opinion, being in love with someone meant being only with them. It was why she never expected anyone to fall in love with her—not with her career she couldn't leave anytime soon.

Maybe that's why you chose a married man to fall in love with? Toby was as unavailable as you and he also had just as big a sacrifice as you to make things work.

Natalie couldn't help but acknowledge the truth. God, she'd been a fool. She also couldn't help but think she'd unconsciously searched for love after fucking so many men who'd wanted only physical release. She'd become desperate for an emotional return too.

She swallowed past the lump in her throat and turned back to Anna. "What about you?"

Anna's smile faded. "I make love to many men, but none of them touch me here." She pressed a fist to her chest. "I can't help but think I'm broken there."

Natalie shook her head. "You're not broken, you're burned out. This life, it makes a woman jaded."

Eloise threw her hands up in the air, almost succeeding this time in toppling over her wine. "Are you girls kidding me? We get paid to have men give us orgasms, paid to enjoy what other women give out for free."

A pair of elderly diners turned in their seats. A gray-haired lady gave them a cold stare even as her companion, a balding, paunchy man, eyed them with barely concealed lust.

Eloise winked at the elderly woman. "You have nothing to worry about. I suspect your husband's wallet is far too light."

Anna ignored the matron's look of horror. Her voice was subdued when she said, "I love sex, don't get me wrong, but I'm... disconnected, even after the best orgasm."

Natalie wanted to hug Anna. "At least you'll never get hurt."

Not emotionally.

Eloise subsided with a sigh. "Natalie's right, you'll keep your heart intact."

"I'm not so sure that's a good thing," Anna said quietly.

Natalie couldn't help but wonder what Anna hid, and why she'd chosen this profession. But some subjects were better not broached. She'd bet every call girl in the VIP Desire Agency had skeletons in their closets they wanted to keep tucked away and out of sight.

Eloise's laugh wasn't jubilant. "All I can say is, I don't plan on letting any man take away my independence, or control me."

Natalie felt something tug inside her for Eloise. The gorgeous woman didn't let much slip, but gaining her freedom after nearly losing it in her home country of Nepal at a young age, had ensured Eloise wouldn't easily give up her independence.

She almost felt sorry for the notorious Wolfe brothers.

She managed a smile as she pushed back her seat. "Thanks girls for sharing lunch with me."

Eloise grimaced. "We haven't exactly cheered you up though."

Natalie shrugged. "At least I know I'm not the only one with problems."

Anna nodded, and sucked down some of her wine. "Kate and Claire have a good life now. It's not impossible we'll get our own love story."

Eloise snorted. "Keep telling yourself that and you might even start to believe it."

Natalie stood. "On that note, I'm going to grab a family-sized meat pie. Then I'm going to eat myself stupid before meeting my new client tonight."

Anna stood too, her eyes shining with concern. "Look after yourself, we don't want to see you being a doormat ever again."

Natalie hugged the young girl. She should be telling Anna to take care of herself too, the petite woman looked too young, too innocent to be in this business.

Instead, Natalie whispered, "Thank you, I will."

Giving Eloise a quick hug, Natalie left behind enough money to cover all their meals, before she stalked out of the restaurant and into the busy Sydney street, half-choked with pedestrians heading to and from lunch.

The clack-clack of her silver high-heels was lost in the noise of traffic and nearby roadwork as she headed in the direction of a bakery that would make a pie that'd be perfect comfort food. But at the prickling sensation between her shoulder blades, she stopped, then turned and peered into the crowd.

She didn't recognize anyone in the sea of people, of course she didn't. She sighed exasperation. The tension inside her was making her overly sensitive and skittish, nothing more. Brushing away the odd sensations, she marched forward and soon lost herself in thoughts about Amos and a growing sense of dread at seeing her new client tonight.

She turned into her destination where scents of freshly baked bread, pies, and cakes caused her belly to churn.

For the first time in her call girl career, she wished she'd never had to rely on her looks. For the first time in her life, she wished a man could desire her more than skin-deep.

A flash of Amos looking at her with assessing eyes—really looking at her, not just her body—sat front and center in her mind. Perhaps it was his interest in the woman beneath that had her question everything lately, made her want more than the empty life she lived.

"Can I help you?"

She nodded at the assistant behind the display case. "I'll have a meat pie... and an apple turnover please," she added.

It would be as good a substitute for hokey pokey ice cream as anything else.

Because maybe food would fill the void inside, at least for a short time.

Chapter Five

Tiffany had tucked Natalie away into the further recesses of her mind by the time the agency town car had dropped her off at the Park Hyatt, where her latest client awaited her. She'd also tucked away all thoughts of Amos, along with the silly fantasies of wishing she'd chosen a different path to the one she'd taken.

If it wasn't for her present lifestyle, her once fiercely independent father would now more than likely be living in an old people's home. Her breath shuddered out. Her father would choose death over that scenario, and being that he was all she had in the world, she wouldn't lose him, not like that. Not for anything.

She approached the reception desk, her head held high and her wildly tousled blonde hair falling down her back. Dressed in an electric blue mini skirt, leather bustier and thigh-high boots, she hoped her client, William Noble, appreciated the untamed look.

She wouldn't dwell on the fact she'd dressed with Amos' approval in mind. He certainly did justice to the untamed look.

After reception handed her the door-card that'd been left for her, she took the elevator to the harbour suite. She sucked in some steadying breaths as the elevator soundlessly took her to her destination. Even her first booking hadn't made her feel this queasy. Like every decision she'd made was ready to smack her upside the head.

The elevator stilled and its doors slid wide apart and she stepped into an elegant sitting room. Taking a moment to compose herself, she knocked twice on the big single door and then stepped back.

The door swung open and she manufactured a seductive smile... a smile that died the moment her eyes connected to the man who stood before her in a white dress shirt and gray slacks. "Amos?" she squeaked.

What the hell? She felt suddenly lightheaded, as though her world was tilting on its axis. But unless Amos had a twin called William, with the same expertly disheveled blond-brown hair, muscly inked biceps, and self-satisfied smile, then she wasn't imagining him.

"Tiffany," he said with a glint in his stare and a twitch to his lips.

"Where's William?" She managed to croak.

Amos' smile disappeared. "I organized another VIP escort to cater to his needs."

She squeezed her eyes shut, vacillating between fury and relief. "You can't micromanage my entire career." She shook her head, her eyes flicking open to view his tall, formidable form. How he managed to look even more imposing dressed in his formal gear was beyond her thought processes right then. "How did you even manage to do that?"

He shrugged, looking completely unfazed. "Money talks."

Which William would have plenty of to even be accepted into the exclusive escort service ran by Maisey.

She exhaled softly, dragging back a little composure. "How much did you have to pay?" She'd bet it was a small fortune to not only appease Maisey, but William too.

"It doesn't matter. What *does* matter is that I get you all to myself." He opened the door wider. "Are you going to come in?"

She arched a brow. "Time is money?"

He smirked. "Kitten, money is the least of my concerns. Time, on the other hand..."

She stepped inside and he shut the door behind them with a decisive clunk. She turned to him. "What exactly is it you want from me?" Her hand lifted and then fell. "Aside from sex?"

In one step, he closed the distance between them, his eyes burning. "As much as the sex is incredible, I *do* want more from you than that."

Her pulse jerked, her belly clenching with both dread and anticipation. "Oh?"

"I'd like to further explore what we have together." His expression sobered. "*But* while you're with me, I have one stipulation."

She pushed aside a flare of rebellion followed as quickly by soul-sucking vulnerability. He paid top dollar for her to do his bidding. She hated that she had to remind herself he was a client, not a lover. "What is it?"

"I don't want any other man garnering your services."

She pressed her lips together. Amos had overheard the conversation she'd had with Harry, had then seen her climb into Harry's car just minutes later. She could hardly blame his proviso.

She nodded. "Of course, that goes without saying."

His expression didn't waver and she had no way of knowing if he believed her or not. Not when he chose not to discuss anything more on the matter.

Instead, he swept out a hand. "Then why don't we enjoy a predinner drink."

So, he was taking her out someplace to eat? She ignored the pang of disappointment. Not being ravished first thing by a client should be a relief for someone of her profession, considering sex was as commonplace as showering morning and night. If only the sex with Amos wasn't so damn earth shatteringly good!

She pasted on a smile. "Thank you, I'd like that."

At the bar was a grand selection of quality spirits and wines and he turned and asked, "Would you like a scotch or perhaps a gin?"

"A gin and tonic would be lovely, thank you."

He poured her a glass and handed it to her before he tipped a generous amount of scotch for himself into a crystal tumbler.

He raised his glass, his eyes glinting under the light. "To an unforgettable night."

She raised her glass, her belly fluttering. "That sounds... ominous."

He tossed back his drink in one swallow, his smoothly-shaven jaw looking stark against his white dress shirt. Somehow he still looked like a rock star, despite his groomed appearance. "Not at all ominous. I'm just keen to do 'normal' things with you."

Her belly lurched between yearning and horror. "Normal as in like a date?"

He put his glass down. "Something like that."

She chugged down her G&T, relishing the burn in her throat. Being with Amos was career suicide. She couldn't afford to fall for another man, couldn't afford to have her heart broken and her spirit crushed.

Amos cocked his head to the side. "Is something troubling you?"

She managed a smile. "No. No, of course not."

His stare sharpened. "Another man, perhaps?"

Heat rose behind her eyes. How did Amos read her so well? Even if she denied it he'd know.

She cleared her throat. "I was recently... hurt by another man."

His jaw tightened. "A client?"

"Yes."

"You still have feelings for him?"

Her laugh came out shaky. She hated discussing Toby, hated knowing what a fool she'd been. "I thought... I loved him."

Did you?

Amos' cheeks hollowed out, as though carved from marble. "I see."

She downed the last of her drink before Amos placed a proprietary hand on her upper arm and walked with her out of the penthouse and into the elevator. She sucked in some much needed oxygen, all too aware of the brooding man beside her... a client whose stare burned her flesh and left her nerve endings sizzling with want.

She sensed he wanted to make her forget about Toby, make her aware only of him even before he spoke.

"Now might not be a good time to tell you how much I'd love to ravage you against the wall, muss up your hair even further, and peel your skirt down your thighs." His voice roughened. "How I'm dying to tear off your thong and lick between the folds of your pussy so I can taste you again."

She refused to look at him; to do so might just be her undoing. And she wasn't about to give in to his wishes and be caught with her pants down... literally.

She instead focused on trying to bring her thudding heart rate down, even as her palms moistened along with her sex. The doors of the elevator slid apart, and as they walked through the lobby, it was only his big hand on the small of her back that kept her upright and not falling on to him.

Minutes later, they were in his stretch limousine and heading toward the heart of Sydney. But she was too distracted to ask where they were eating. Not when his big, warm hand drifted beneath her skirt, his rough palm moving up and down her thigh.

Her lips parted right along with her legs. She stared with hungry eyes at the wedge of his arousal in his pants. Damn, she'd never wanted a man so badly.

His thumb stroked along the edge of the material of her thong, his stare lingering on her mouth when he said hoarsely, "Should I tell you what I'd like you to do to me right now?"

Her mouth dried with anticipation even as she looked up at him and asked, "How long have we got?"

"Long enough."

She did a slow lick of her lips before she grasped the fly of his slacks and carefully slid it undone. His hand dropped away from her thigh before he lifted his hips. She dragged his pants down along with his boxer briefs, releasing his swollen cock. She sighed appreciatively. There was surely nothing hotter than a well-endowed man. His pink cockhead glistened with the smallest bead of pre-cum, and she swooped down to lick it from his slit.

She barely heard his harsh intake of breath. Not when his salty essence tingled and danced on her tongue, leaving her wanting so much more. She pulled the head of his cock into her mouth, circling the velvet skin with her tongue and shivering with delight at hearing his low moan.

Damn. She wanted this man with everything she had.

Suctioning his shaft further inside her mouth, she took him to the back of her throat and held him there for a few tongue-swirling seconds before she retreated and then took him in again. She scraped her teeth along his vein-roped shaft and his moan turned into a raspy growl.

She cupped his balls in a hand, gently kneading even as she bobbed her head faster, devouring as much of his length as humanly possible and drinking in his musky scent. Oral sex might be a part of her job description, but she'd never wanted to please a man as much as she did Amos, never wanted to taste the grand finale like she did with him.

His hands curled into her hair as his balls suddenly tightened. He was close, and she knew just how to push him over the line. She nipped his pulsating flesh and his seed erupted. He tasted like heaven.

"Jesus." He groaned, his hands loosening and then stroking her head.

She released him after she'd drank every last drop, and straightened, her eyes searching his dazed stare. "I think it's safe to say you enjoyed that as much as I did."

He secured his boxer briefs and pants over his softening cock. Blowing out a slow breath, his heavy-lidded gaze returned to her mouth. "When I said we'd have an unforgettable night, I wasn't thinking only about the sex."

"It's what I'm good at... what you pay me for."

All slumbering satisfaction slid off him like water from a sheet of glass. "I know you want men to see you as a sex object, but I'm thinking there's a whole lot more depth to you than that. I *know* there is."

Her chin tilted. "Maybe you're right. But it's not what you pay me for, is it?"

He frowned, but when the stretch limo slowed, he rasped, "We're here."

He escorted her toward a dingy little brick building on the corner of the busy city street. Inside the building was no bigger or better, but what it lacked in size it made up for in character. A wood-paneled bar ran the length of the back of the room and, nearby, a piano tinkled out a jazz song while patrons took up the bar stools and deep sunken lounges.

Amos put his arm around her and guided her down some thick wooden stairs to a dark underground room where candles flickered on round tables with crimson tablecloths. Most of the tables were already full, but Amos had reserved their place right near a stage at the front.

Once the skimpily dressed waitress in a ruffled black miniskirt and cut-off white blouse, left them with their menus, Tiffany looked around the room with excitement buzzing deep in her belly.

"This is all so exciting," she said, turning to him with a smile.

His teeth glinted along with his eyes behind the candlelight. "I was hoping you'd like it."

She leaned forward, her hand curling around his thigh. Even under his slacks she felt his muscles clench in response. "You come here often?"

"No, it's my first time too. But, after hearing all the hype, I promised myself I'd take someone special here with me one day."

He was calling her *special.*

Warmth radiated through her chest and she was left feeling giddy with joy and stupid hope. "I'm glad it was me you chose to bring here."

His hand enveloped hers on his thigh. "I couldn't imagine experiencing this with anyone else."

He bent his head and she leaned even closer for a slow, lingering kiss. Though what they shared wasn't openly passionate in the shadowy, but crowded, room, their intimacy was startling. She pulled back, wondering if her eyes shone as clearly as his did. This didn't feel at all like what a client and an escort shared, not one bit.

"Are you okay?" he asked.

She nodded. "Of course."

She bit into her bottom lip. It wouldn't do to let him know how precarious their relationship was getting. It was only with Toby that she had allowed her feelings to slip, and had then lived to regret it. She straightened in her seat, putting distance between them. She wouldn't go through an emotional rollercoaster, not a second time.

She doubted her heart would recover.

The back of her neck prickled again, and she breathed in slow and deep even as she fought off the urge to peer around and find whoever watched them from the shadows. In her kind of work, gaining a stalker wasn't anything new. But if she let Maisey in on her suspicions, she had no doubt the madam would instantly sic her chauffeur-come-occasional-bodyguard onto Tiffany.

That was the very last thing she wanted.

"Are you sure you're okay?" Amos repeated.

She used every bit of her acting abilities to send him a full-wattage smile. She then used even more of that ability to withdraw her hand from his thigh when everything in her yearned for the connection.

The cabaret show started and her pulse returned to normal. Her shoulders relaxed and her stomach muscles unclenched. She'd never be safer or more secure with a man like Amos. It was time to enjoy the show.

Chapter Six

Amos probably should have concentrated on the cabaret show a little more, but it was next to impossible for him to notice anyone but Tiffany. He had no idea what it was that drew him to her, but her allure was irresistible.

He'd always had a weakness for blondes, but that had little to nothing to do with the way he felt about her. She was the whole package. Beautiful, sweet but sassy, with an edge of vulnerability that he occasionally glimpsed beneath her strength and the shell she'd built around her heart.

He took a swallow of his scotch. What he'd do to crack into that shell and expose the woman he so desperately wanted to get to know.

The scantily clad waitress placed their plate of food in front of them. He nodded thanks, but wasn't even slightly tempted by the pork cutlets with garlic scalloped potatoes and green beans.

He hid a smile when Tiffany ate her dinner with gusto, her expression animated as she watched the show, in-between sliding him furtive glances he couldn't fail but notice. Of course he noticed; he hadn't looked anywhere else but at her since being here.

Still, he'd also picked up an odd vibe from her and, for a moment, thought she might be having a panic attack. Her pinched, pale face and wide eyes had immediately alerted him. Lord only knew he'd suffered them enough times as a child after his parents had died in a car crash, which he'd survived.

Music had become his life saver, and given him the strength needed to push past his anxieties.

But not everyone was as lucky.

Perhaps Tiffany didn't like overcrowded, small spaces like this one? Except not even a minute after he'd asked if she was okay, her anxiety had dissipated like smoke into the air.

He cut and then pronged a piece of his pork chop and chewed it thoughtfully. He'd keep an eye on her and make sure she didn't succumb to any deep-rooted phobias she might carry around. Because the one thing he wanted more than anything, aside from the woman in question, was to take care of her.

The show carried on without his attention. His gaze strayed back time and time again to Tiffany's profile, noting the delicate but aristocratic sweep of her nose, her high cheekbones and jutting chin, framed to perfection by her long, expertly mussed silver-blonde hair. She was every artist's wet dream, a beautiful woman who stimulated every part of him, including his muse.

His stare dipped to her naughty outfit, one he couldn't wait to later peel off her body. His dick jerked against the seam of his pants and he resisted an urge to reposition his anatomy into a more comfortable position.

Evidently having Tiffany suck him dry wasn't near enough. He wanted to plunge between her thighs, then turn her around and take her from behind, his balls slapping her ass and his fingers speared through her hair.

Everyone at the tables suddenly clapped and hollered as the cabaret show ended. At least he didn't have to stifle his aroused groan. The dancers and singers on stage took their bows, before Tiffany turned to him with a flushed face and bright eyes. "That was fantastic."

Was it?

He dipped his head in agreement. "A great show."

She arched a disbelieving brow. "So which part of the cabaret was your favorite?"

He grinned, not even pretending interest. "This bit now where they're all bowing and about to leave the stage."

"Well you missed a great show."

He shrugged. "I preferred the scenery over here."

She didn't drop her stare, but he noted the twin flags of color on her cheeks. He'd bet she rarely blushed, and it was pleasing to know he had that effect on her.

She glanced at his plate. "You're not hungry either?"

He looked down. Damn. He'd had one bite of his pork and that was it. Evidently he really had been too distracted by Tiffany and the washing machine cycle of his thoughts.

He shrugged. "I only eat when I'm hungry." He leaned forward and murmured, "And right now the only thing I want to sample is between your thighs."

Her breath hissed, a deeper tinge of pink washing over her cheeks and her eyes glittering. "You sound like the big, bad wolf, about to eat me."

He stood. "Then let's get out of here, Little Red Riding Hood."

She giggled, snaring his hand as she stood too, before following his long-legged stride around the tables and chairs and up the stairs. He knew he was rushing her, but he legitimately couldn't get her home fast enough—the journey was already going to take way too long—and completely corrupt her.

But the moment he hit the ground floor level, he froze.

He tore his stare away from the woman at the bar to focus on Tiffany. "Kitten, would you mind waiting at one of the lounges for a minute?"

Curiosity shone from her eyes, but she didn't ask questions and, for the first and undoubtedly only time, he was glad she was a call girl and not his girlfriend. Glad she knew better than to question his every move.

Tiffany nodded. "Sure."

The moment she sank into the nearest, squishy lounge, he strode over to Jasmine. The dark-haired woman sat languidly on a bar stool, facing their way, idly stirring her green drink with a cocktail umbrella.

He bit back a curse. Damn it to hell, he couldn't keep being the nice guy to fucked-up women because of his mother's death. He couldn't be responsible for this woman's well-being because guilt still riddled him for not saving his mother.

"What the hell are you doing, following me here?" He scowled down at her.

She blinked up at him and beneath her innocent eyes lurked the damaged soul he prayed wouldn't hurt anyone he knew. Her cloying perfume drifted to him, reminding him of picked roses that'd sat too long in the sun.

"Don't you mean, what are you doing here with *her*?" She angled her head toward Tiffany, a flare of unfettered jealousy leaking from her stare.

He moved to stand between Tiffany and Jasmine. "She was my date for the night. Not that it's any of your business."

"Liar!" She pulled free a folded piece of newspaper from inside her bra, unfolding it with savage hands before holding it up for him to see. "You were with her last night too." She sucked in a shuddering breath. "Did you ever look at me like you look at her?"

Amos stared at the photo and article that'd been printed by the local rag in record time. Damn it all to hell, he'd completely forgotten about the flash that'd gone off last night at his afterparty. The picture revealed his obsession with Tiffany as he looked down at her while they danced. He genuinely looked as if he was ready to fuck her and slide a wedding ring on her finger all at the same time.

He shrugged, striving for casual. "What can I say, a photo doesn't lie."

Jasmine tucked the article back into her bra with exaggerated care, before she sucked some of the green liquor up her straw. "I don't recall you *ever* looking at any of your other dates the way you do with this one." She sighed. "She *is* beautiful, I'll give her that, but you must know she's nothing but a filthy little whore."

His hands clenched involuntarily, his teeth gritting against an urge to hurl abuse. It would be just what this psychopath wanted. And though Tiffany might well be a whore, she was the most beautiful woman inside and out he'd ever had the fortune to know. "Stay away from her."

Jasmine giggled, but it wasn't anything joyous. "Wow. You really do have it bad for her."

She turned and placed her empty glass onto the bar with a sharp clack. She twisted back to face him, her lips curling with distaste. She looked more like a witch than she did the gorgeous girl his body had once responded to.

Once, being the operative word.

She slowly crossed her boot-clad legs. "You know I can't let you be with her." At his rushed exhalation, she leaned toward him, showing off her generous cleavage as she added, "You're mine. You've always been mine. You just haven't realized it yet."

There was no reasoning with this woman, she was barely even sane. "No, I'm not yours, and never will be." He'd protect Tiffany from this madwoman with his life if need be. "Now leave me the hell alone, and go find yourself some other poor bastard to harass."

"You know you can't be with her twenty-four seven."

"Don't bet on it," he ground out the words.

He leaned forward this time, no longer caring about Jasmine's fragile mental state. All he cared about was Tiffany, and absolutely no one threatened her.

"If I see you near her again, don't think I won't do whatever it takes to protect her."

Jasmine blanched, her eyes glittering with helpless rage. "Are you threatening me?"

He hid a grimace of distaste. She clearly didn't like it when the shoe was on the other foot. He straightened. "Touch even one hair on her head and you'll discover I'm a man of my word."

He twisted away from the women he could barely stomach. But as he made his way back to Tiffany, Jasmine said loud enough for him to hear, "We're meant to be together."

~

Tiffany ignored the burning eyes of the dark-haired woman who'd monopolized Amos' time, even as a ripple of unease moved up and down her spine. Something didn't feel right about that woman. Or maybe Tiffany was just being overprotective and a little bit... jealous.

But of course he'd have attractive women just like the brunette after him at every turn; it was his due as a famous rock star.

"Another rabid fan?" she asked as he stopped in front of her.

"Something like that."

She hid a frown as she stood. Something definitely wasn't right. But as he put an arm around her waist and led her to the exit doors, her concerns faded as she melted against him and luxuriated in their closeness.

In the chauffeured limo she snuggled even closer and tilted back her head to accept his light kisses that suggested much deeper, fiercer ones to come. She shivered. No matter her growing feelings for this man, she'd do her job and do it well, and enjoy the short time she'd have with him. Not to mention take pleasure in the fact the faceless William had been replaced with Amos.

He curled his arm around her and she wilted against his strength. Tiredness swamped over her and she was half-asleep by the time the limousine slowed down and Amos murmured, "We're here."

She climbed out and stood gawping at the building, which looked more like a warehouse than any home she'd seen. "This is where you live?" She squeaked.

He grinned. "Appearances can be deceiving."

She clasped his upper arm and he shortened his stride as he walked up steps and approached a big wooden door. Unlocking it and swinging it open, he flicked a switch and half a dozen lights fizzed into being on the high beamed ceiling above them.

Her eyes widened. A huge stainless steel kitchen took up residence on a far wall. A lounge area with red leather modular chairs faced a huge flat screen television. A big red and black swirling rug softened the marble-look polished concrete floor.

The floor was a huge expanse, dotted here and there by interesting art sculptures, large vases and square tables. And behind some latticed artwork, she made out gym equipment: weights, a treadmill, punching bag, and bench press.

"You'd get lost in here," she said, turning to him.

He nodded. "I like my space, and being that I work in the city, coming home is something I look forward to every night. A place to stretch out, unwind, and relax."

"I bet."

He grinned. "Come, I'll show you my loft."

"Your bedroom?"

He nodded. "There's that, yes, but I also have my office up there."

Heading toward the acrylic staircase, she looked up at the floor above, which took up less than a third of the space of the ground floor. It left the rest of the vaulted ceiling free, giving a sense of limitless space.

She followed him upstairs and into a good sized sitting room that reminded her of an indoor patio. She smiled. She could imagine him sitting up here, drinking a coffee and surveying his domain.

He opened his carved wooden bedroom door. A big skylight overhead showcased the night sky with its scattering of twinkling stars. She could also imagine lying on his huge, four-poster king bed and looking up into deep space.

"I love it."

He stepped behind her, his arms going around her waist. "I never wanted to share this with anyone, until now."

She twisted in his embrace and looked up at him. The lights in the open area splashed just a little illumination inside his bedroom, but it was enough to witness the serious glint in his stare.

"You've never brought anyone here before?"

He shook his head. "Never. Not even my band members. This is my separation from everything business."

"No... girlfriends?"

"No. Only you."

She blinked, feeling discombobulated and out of sorts. No wonder he'd taken her to a hotel the first night.

"I'm flattered."

"Mm. And I want nothing more than to ravish you right now."

"Then what's stopping you?" Damn, was the high-pitched voice really hers?

"Nothing will stop me, but not here. I've made arrangements to take you elsewhere."

She frowned. It had to be ten or eleven o'clock at night, where could he possibly take her now?

He grinned at seeing her confusion. "Come on, I'll show you."

She followed him out of his bedroom, past the sitting room and another closed door which had to be his office, to narrow treads that led to a trapdoor in the ceiling. Amos took to the steps like he'd done it a thousand times before, pushing the trapdoor up and stepping through.

He took her hand as she stepped onto the flat roof, and she pressed her other hand to her mouth at seeing the big, dark helicopter sitting on the roof like a lazy, overgrown dragonfly.

"Here's our ride," Amos said, amusement filling his voice.

A strange feeling of unreality came over her, like the scene was playing out for someone else, someone far more fortunate. Someone worthy of this sort of attention.

She turned to him. “Are you serious?”

He grinned and nodded. “Yes.” He clasped her hand and stepped toward the flying beast. “I couldn’t be more serious.”

Chapter Seven

The helicopter pilot set the machine down in a big paddock, twenty or so yards away from a house with a wraparound veranda encased in a grape vine.

Tiffany curled her fists together under her chin, and yelled above the noise of the spinning rotors, "Where are we?"

Amos' eyes sparkled. "Welcome to inland Victoria, and my holiday home. A place I retreat to whenever I crave fresh air and the great outdoors." His mouth curled wryly. "And of course safety away from rabid fans."

Someone had left the house lights on, probably a caretaker, and she could see inside the windows through the sheer curtains. A small fire glowed in the fireplace, and a bowl of fruit sat on round wooden table with a lacy white tablecloth. Pots and pans hung on hooks above a gleaming kitchen bench. It looked homely and inviting.

"It's lovely."

They climbed out of the helicopter, ducking low and running clear from the whirling blades. Amos gave a thumbs-up to the pilot, and the machine roared as it pulled back up into the air.

She laughed, exhilarated by the flight and the wind that now whipped at her hair and pushed dust into their faces. Even so, the air filling her lungs was cleaner, fresher than the city smog.

Amos chuckled beside her, the chopper noise already fading as he said, "You make everything seem so fresh and new again."

"I doubt I'd ever get jaded flying in that thing."

The millions of city lights and then the random twinkling lights of farmhouses spread out intermittently across the land had been stark contrast. As had the Opera House, Harbour Bridge, and tall buildings that had given way to the shadowy outlines of mountains and the glint of rivers and dams under the moonlight.

He curled an arm around her waist and she sighed against his shoulder as they traversed the yard, where crickets chirped and a bat shrieked somewhere in the distance. She sucked in a breath of the clean-as-clean air, thrilled to be here; a part of Amos' life just for a little while longer.

The outside chill was tempered immediately by the fire inside, and Tiffany stepped across the polished timber floor toward the small flames behind the bricked off grate. She stretched her hands to the heat. "I can't remember the last time I enjoyed a real fireplace."

Amos stood beside her. "It's nice to get away from the city and experience something so natural, isn't it?"

She turned to him, her voice husky. "If this is normal then I never want to go back to crazy again."

His stare held hers. "You'd give up your lifestyle for this?"

In a heartbeat.

She couldn't tell Amos the truth. Couldn't let him know why she worked as an escort. If she didn't do what she did, then her father wouldn't have the modified house and round the clock care she needed. She also wouldn't be able to see him most days.

She kept her personal life strictly private for good reason. It was a way of keeping hold of who she really was and of protecting her heart. She'd opened herself up to Toby too soon and look where that had left her. Even though being with Amos made her realize how right things could be between two people, she wasn't trusting so easily again.

"I'm guessing that's a no, then?"

She blinked, gathering back her scattered thoughts.

Her voice came out brittle with her lie. "Do you really think I could give up the city lifestyle, the parties and dinners, the shopping and pampering, for this?"

He didn't frown, but disappointment was stamped all over his face. "To be honest, yeah, I did."

Her belly gave a peculiar little twist. He understood her so well. Playing the escort-client game was going to be harder with him because he dug deeper than her other clients. He actually wanted to know the real her, not the sexy siren men paid to keep them satisfied.

"It's late," he finally said into a silence broken by the faint crackle of burning wood. "Let's shower and get some sleep."

She nodded, and followed him down the hallway. "You know I didn't bring a change of clothes."

His laugh melted her insides even before he said, "You won't need clothes for what I have in mind."

In the bathroom, he turned the taps on and adjusted the pressure. She loved watching the play of his back muscles through his shirt, admired his naturally streaked brown-blond hair that sat unfashionably long past his collar. Warmth radiated off his skin, and she sucked in his musky, aroused scent like it was her very last breath.

She shuddered with need. It was all she could do not to rip his clothes off him even before he twisted back to face her.

Steam filled the air, saturating them with moisture as he cupped her face, his lips gentle on hers as he kissed her, savored her. Her breasts were heavy and her nipples sharp points behind her bustier when he finally pulled away.

His eyes glowed, his cock bulging in his pants. Every angle and plane in his face was stamped with need. Yet it was almost methodical the way they pulled off their footwear before they helped each other out of their clothes and tossed them into the hamper next to the shower stall.

There was nothing disciplined about the desire that built like a furnace between them. Nothing even remotely controlled about their kiss when they came together in the shower, their mouths merging as one and their hands all over one another.

She gasped into his mouth when he slid a finger into her pussy, his thumb plucking her clit like he was playing her in the same way he played his guitar. She was already in tune for him, and beyond willing and ready for his mastery. But he continued strumming her fleshy little knot of nerves, continued to push a finger, then two, in and out of her.

She was careening toward orgasm faster than she could gain her breath, teetering on the edge even before his mouth left hers and he dropped onto his knees. Her breath hissed when he parted the folds of her labia. He looked up at her under the billowing steam and the water coursing over them, before he leaned forward, his mouth latching onto her inner flesh with unbearable skill.

His tongue flicked even as he suckled, and he pressed an outspread hand on the flat plane of her belly to help hold her in place as her legs shook and her body turned into liquid.

His mouth on her pussy was pleasurable enough, but seeing his head between her thighs and his stare watching her every reaction pushed the barometer way past the boiling point.

He sucked harder and she didn't even try and fight against the powerful rush of sensation hurtling through her body. The climax took away her will to resist this man even a second longer. She put a hand on her mouth to stifle the scream of rapture, stifle his name that she called out as pleasure ricocheted through her in a tsunami before leaving her weak and defenseless.

He straightened then, before he picked her up and spun her around against the wall. He kissed her again, pushing his tongue into her mouth and sharing her musky scent, before his cock, which throbbed against her belly, was suddenly at her core.

She stiffened a nanosecond before he pushed the length of his shaft deep inside her. She groaned. It was too late to worry about unprotected sex, too late to worry about anything but wrapping her legs around his hips and losing herself in his powerful strokes that moved faster and faster, until she was tipped right over the edge again and he followed seconds after.

The steam billowed around them when she finally found the strength to uncurl her legs from his hips and step onto the tiles on weak spaghetti-legs. It wasn't the steam that put moisture in her eyes when she looked up at him.

His eyes flashed, his jaw tightening. "We didn't use protection, I know." He lifted a hand and drew the back of his knuckles along her jaw. "I'm to blame for getting so carried away."

She sighed. "I'm at fault too." After all, her it was also her job to ensure her client always wore a condom.

He shook his head. "It was mine, one hundred percent. But just so you know," he rasped, "I'm clean."

"As am I."

His eyebrows furrowed. "You're on the pill though, yeah?"

"Of course."

His thumb brushed her lip. "You know, you'd make beautiful babies."

Her throat thickened, and her voice came out hoarse. "As would you."

She ignored a frisson of pain at the thought of him making beautiful babies with his future wife. The envy wasn't helped knowing she'd never get to experience motherhood. Not in her line of work. Besides, children were expensive, she couldn't afford to raise a family and look after her father's huge medical finances as well.

Amos flipped off the taps and they stepped outside the shower stall. Using a soft, fluffy towel that smelled of lavender, she stood still as he blotted all the moisture from her skin. Warmth rushed through her veins as he took extra care drying her hardening breasts and sensitized nipples, before he bent to pay attention drying the lips of her pussy.

Her knees began to quake, heat centering at her core, when she drew the towel out of his hands and dried him in return. She took great pleasure in running the towel over his wide shoulders and along his pecs, before rubbing it down the trail of hair leading from his navel to his cock.

It was an odd kind of thrill, considering how regularly she witnessed a man's desire, to see Amos' cock harden all over again. Even odder was her strong urge to take him once more in her mouth.

His big hand wrapped around her upper arm and tugged her fully upright. His eyes glowed. "You're killing me," he growled.

When he claimed her lips with his own in a slow, tender kiss that revealed iron willpower, her yearning intensified. But not for sex, she wanted all of Amos. His heart, his soul... everything.

He pulled back and she followed him into the master bedroom, where they both climbed naked into the big bed with its midnight coverlet. He turned her to him and wrapped her in his arms, but their skin-on-skin contact didn't progress into sex. He was evidently content to simply hold her. And damned if that didn't make her heart completely melt.

She woke the next morning, blinking against the natural light flooding into the bedroom and realizing she was still Tiffany, not Natalie. She'd do well to remember that and not make her time with Amos personal.

She eased herself out of his arms and turned to watch him slumber. This waking up beside him and then watching him sleep was getting into a bit of a habit. One she didn't mind repeating.

Her lips curved into a wondrous smile as lightness spread through her chest. The man might be a livewire when he performed on stage and in the bedroom, but he knew how to sleep when it was needed too.

She stretched her arms above her head, aware her tiredness was more fulfilling than exhausting. Long hours of sex with Amos hadn't left her wrung out like dishrag. It'd left her warmly satisfied and wanting more.

But then she couldn't remember a deeper or more relaxed sleep in a very long time. Being in Amos' arms made her feel safe and secure. She squeezed her eyes closed. Made her feel things she'd been trying to avoid. The last thing she needed was to get burned by another client.

Padding away from the bed, she stepped into the bedroom's walk-in-closet and found a white unisex robe. Shrugging it on, she walked through the house and outside to its back veranda.

The house really did sit in the middle of nowhere, with distant mountains and a far-off fence line framing an otherwise flat landscape of green grass. She breathed in the fresh air, lifting her face to the warmth of the sun and admiring the clear azure sky.

She of all people understood Amos' need for space and the peace and quiet that came with it. Sleeping with regular clients didn't make her feel like they were any less of a stranger. It was still casual sex, and they were still nothing more than men who'd leave her in bed without looking back. It was enough to wish for a whole different life, a simple life, like being here.

A kookaburra laughed, drawing her attention to the one lone tree that shaded a shed off to the side of the house. Before her father's accident she'd lived with him in a semi-rural area, enjoying nature but with shopping centers, restaurants, and cinemas only a handful of minutes down the road.

Being here reminded her how much she loved the great outdoors, the crisp, clean air and the uncluttered space spread out around her for miles.

She smelled the tantalizing aroma of coffee minutes before Amos stepped outside in old jeans and a white t-shirt. Her mouth dried. He looked rugged and too damn masculine for her peace of mind, even with a steaming mug of coffee in each hand.

"I come bearing gifts."

She smiled at his dry humor, before she accepted the mug and took a sip. "Thank you." She tried not to notice the way the white shirt hugged his powerful torso and set off his inked arms. "When I got up you were sound asleep."

He shrugged. "What can I say? My body seems to know when you're not near me."

She grinned. "That's because your body loves sex."

His eyes glinted with a far more serious look. "Or maybe it's simply that I love being with you."

Chapter Eight

Tiffany refused to read more into Amos' words than what he'd meant. Loved being with her didn't equate to being in love with her. And yet she swore the intensity in his eyes told her otherwise.

Before she could drum up something halfway intelligent, he took a sip of his coffee and looked out over the endless green grass, a hand casually anchored on his hip. "I love being here with you even more."

She bit the inside of her cheek. Was it possible his feelings for her were real? Dare she even hope they were? She blew out a slow breath. No, it was better to keep things strictly professional and uncomplicated. As much as every cell in her body hummed with a need to lean on Amos, she refused to give in to that foolish desire.

What man in his right mind would even consider taking on the financial burden she faced day in, day out? Amos might be wealthy, but he wasn't stupid. No man would want to commit to that sort of a responsibility.

But she considered herself lucky to afford her lifestyle and that of her father's. When the insurance for her dad's accident had fallen through, she'd had to quit university and find employment fast. The VIP Escort Agency had been the only high-paying profession available.

Becoming an escort had been a godsend, even if her growing anxiety levels told her otherwise.

She glanced his way and said huskily, "Thank you. I love being here with you too. It's nice to get away from the traffic, the chaos, and the noise."

He nodded. "We're in the fertile valley of the Lochte Mountains, we couldn't be further away from the concrete jungle if we tried." He waved a hand toward the highest point of the distant mountains, his voice becoming quiet. "My father and I used to hike those mountains. It's another reason I bought this property, and why I built a cabin up there where we camped."

She held onto that tidbit of information, yearning to know so much more about him.

He turned to her. "I'd like to take you up there after breakfast."

She nodded. "I'd like that too."

He smiled. "Good, it's settled then. Finish your coffee and I'll make some breakfast. How does bacon and eggs sound?"

Her belly chose that moment to grumble. She laughed. "Apparently, it sounds perfect."

His stare lingered on her face, as though he wasn't in any hurry to leave her. Warmth radiated through her. How many men had ever looked at her like that, as though she was the only woman in the world for them, and not just in the bedroom?

No one, that she was aware. Men loved to look at her, to fuck her, nothing more.

Perhaps because that's all you're offering?

Her smile died, but she refused to allow self-doubts to spoil the moment. Out here, away from other people, it seemed as if they really did have all the time in the world and she, for one, wasn't in any hurry to get back to reality.

Except you'll have another client tonight.

Tension sucked away the last of her joy and settled into stiff lines across her shoulders. Since being with Amos, she was starting to dread being with another man. He made all her other clients pale in comparison. She only hoped he'd somehow managed to book her for tonight as well and that she wouldn't be sleeping with anyone but him.

"Is something wrong?" Amos asked, his eyes assessing.

She shook her head. "No. I'm good, thanks."

"Something wiped that beautiful smile right off your face."

She bit into her bottom lip. "I was thinking about where I'd be tonight."

His face gentled even as something possessive flashed in his stare. "You'll be here again with me, in my arms."

Her eyes widened, her breath for a moment catching in her throat. "Maisey allowed you another night with me?"

He shrugged. "Like I said, money talks." He spun on his heel. "You're welcome to join me in the kitchen when you're ready."

She stared after him as his long-legged stride took him all too quickly from the veranda and out of sight. She glanced away. She was all too aware she could feast her eyes on him all day long.

Her breath huffed out. She had to remember she was living in a fantasy world right now. Not in the real world where clients awaited her in expensive hotel rooms, and where her father's medical bills piled high until she paid out another big installment.

She turned back to the endless landscape. For the moment, she'd enjoy being here with Amos. For the moment, she'd forget all about the hardships of life and give into the urge to bury her head in the sand. Besides, if her father needed her she was only a phone call away, he'd survive without her for a few days.

She drank the rest of her coffee, squared her shoulders, and followed Amos back inside. She wouldn't waste a minute more questioning her every decision.

Fifteen minutes later, she pushed her half-full plate away, patting her drum-tight belly. "I think you're trying to fatten me up."

He chuckled and reached for her plate to eat what she hadn't. "Kitten, thin or thick, you're perfect in my eyes."

She blinked and gave him a little smile. "Little wonder you're such a great songwriter."

He looked up. "Oh?"

"You know just the right things to say to a person."

He reached over and clasped her hand on the table. "I write songs from my heart. The same goes with what I say."

She looked down at their hands. Maybe it was time to also lay the cards on the table. "I'm a call girl, an escort you pay for sex and social engagements. Our relationship is strictly business."

If she expected anger or even flat out refusal, she sure as hell hadn't expected his bark of laughter. His hand tightened on hers even as he shook his head. "My god, you sound like an auto recording, a spiel you save for particularly bothersome clients."

Her body tensed. "I'm sorry it came across like a joke."

He sighed. "Don't be mad at me, kitten. The truth is, even if I wanted a relationship, I can't be in one."

Odd how that piece of news was exactly what she needed to hear, yet it made her feel... deflated. She cleared her throat. "Work commitments?"

"Something like that."

She managed a nod. "Then I'm glad we've cleared that up."

Amos placed his fork carefully onto his plate, his expression brooding. "Yeah, me too."

The distant whomp-whomp sound of a helicopter grew in volume, and Amos scraped his chair back and stood. "The clothes I ordered for you are finally here."

She stood too. "Wait. What?"

"C'mon and I'll show you."

Twenty minutes later, Tiffany stood in front of the dresser mirror in Amos' bedroom. The clothes he'd ordered in the nearest town and which had been picked up via helicopter fit her perfectly. From the dozen or so outfits, she'd chosen light colored denim jeans, an aqua cotton long-sleeved shirt and tan ankle boots.

As for the underwear, she had her choice of dozens of Victoria's Secret little scraps of silk and lace, not to mention lingerie. She sighed.

The one thing she loved to indulge in was expensive bras and panties. There was nothing quite like the perfect body-hugging fit of a thong or sexy bra.

She pulled her hair back and tied it into a knot on top of her head. She grinned. If she added an Akubra hat, she might even pass for a cowgirl.

Amos stepped into the bedroom and whistled approval. "I'm starting to believe you could wear a sack and still look gorgeous."

"There you go again, saying all the right things." She looked at him from the mirror's reflection. "A girl just might get used to it, you know."

He approached her in a couple of easy strides, his hands encircling her waist from behind. When he bent and kissed the back of her bared neck, she shivered with need.

"A girl could get used to a lot of things around you," she added with a croak.

He lifted his head, his eyes gleaming in the mirror. "Is that such a bad thing?"

She inhaled sharply. "Whatever happened to not wanting a relationship?"

His stare held hers. "Maybe I'm getting well and truly over someone else trying to dictate my life."

She frowned. Who the hell held such sway over him? His band? His manager? His legion of fans?

His hands tightened on her waist momentarily before he loosened his hold with a sigh. "Look, why don't we forget about everything today but enjoying ourselves."

She nodded. It wasn't her place to question Amos' motives, even if she had to remind herself that every time she was with him. "Okay."

She turned to him and he took hold of her hand, leading her outside to a shed where a shiny, red off-road quad bike was parked.

"This is our ride?" she asked, grinning from ear-to-ear as butterflies danced in her belly.

She'd never ridden on any type of bike before, and she didn't mind having an excuse to wrap her arms around his waist.

He grinned in return. "It sure is."

He handed her a helmet and helped tighten her chin straps. Her skin shivered as his callused hands brushed her neck.

He put his own helmet on. "Ready?" he asked in a voice that sounded far away behind the confines of his headgear.

She nodded and he started the machine before she climbed behind him and placed her booted feet on the back foot pegs. Within minutes they'd left the house far behind, the wind whipping past them and the sun warming her back.

She turned her head to the side and leaned against his strong back, watching the blue sky and the vivid green ground skate past. A woman really could get used to this life. Her hands tightened around his waist. But only a fool would make the same mistake twice.

She lifted her legs with a shriek when a striped orange snake slithered out of their way.

Amos turned his head and yelled. "A tiger snake, harmless if you leave them alone."

Deadly if you didn't.

She could probably learn something from that.

Half an hour later, Amos was maneuvering the quad up the start of an incline, where a faint track weaved its way around eucalyptus trees, fallen branches, and large, moss covered rocks. The big, white-trunked trees with their leafy branches allowed dappled sunlight through, where yellow butterflies danced in the late morning warmth, and birds flitted through the high canopy.

He rode the bike with a skill that allowed her to simply enjoy the solitude and the glorious vistas the higher they ascended. Far below, his house sat in the middle of the vast expanse of green, smoke lightly billowing from its rooftop in the breeze.

A goanna scuttled from a patch of sun on the track ahead, its tongue flickering in and out before it moved with a fast, ungainly gait out of their way and climbed the nearest tree with ease.

The track sharpened and she clung to Amos a little tighter. She mightn't be a farm girl, but she was well aware of the danger of four-wheelers on steeper terrain, where they could easily upend. But Amos didn't falter, his riding sure and confident, and her nerves dissipated long before they topped the rise and she saw the cabin ahead.

He pulled the quad to the side of the building and she dismounted and removed her helmet, caring less that her hair probably stuck out like a birds nest as she took in the view behind the cabin. "That's spectacular."

Amos took her helmet and placed it on the quad's seat with his own. He turned back to her with a grin, his delight all too evident as he too surveyed the sweeping views. "It's about as close to being a bird as we'll get without actually flying."

She walked with him to the back of the cabin and stepped up onto the huge deck. Her heart skipped a couple of beats as she walked to the edge and looked down at the void below. "Wow."

Amos stood behind her, his big arms encircling her waist as though preventing her from falling. "It puts things into perspective, doesn't it," he murmured.

She leaned back against him, soaking in his strength, his... purity. She blinked, for a moment not seeing the glorious sweep of green far below. It seemed incredible that out of all the men she'd met, including smooth-talking Toby, it was a rock star who revealed a clean soul and a heart of gold.

She swallowed past the thickness in her throat, and said, "It sure does."

They stayed that way for some time, Amos seemingly needing her in his arms as much as she needed his arms around her.

She only moved when he murmured, "Let's go inside, there's something I want to show you."

She followed him through the glass sliding doors, surprised by how much bigger the cabin was inside than it looked from the exterior. A basic kitchen with big windows to let in the sunlight and take advantage of the views, and a lounge with faded recliners and a couple of squishy beanbags centered around a fireplace.

"No television?" she asked.

"No. This is my escape from civilization." He took hold of her hand and led her past the lounge and toward a closed door. "It's also where I write a lot of my songs."

He swung open the door and she stepped into the large room which was clearly a recording studio. She recognized a few pieces, from a mixing desk and computer, audio interface, microphones on stands, headphones hanging from wall hooks and a dozen cables snaking from one thing to another.

Amos revealed a few of the things she didn't recognize, from bass traps to acoustic panels, diffusers and monitor isolation pads on stands. "It's only a basic setup compared to the recording studio Frankenstein's Blood often uses, but it's everything I want at my fingertips."

She nodded. "It looks like the perfect place to chill and write music."

He nodded. "It is." He took a guitar off its stand and plucked a few notes, before he looked up at said, "Want to hear a bit of my latest song?"

Her breath stalled in her throat. Any fan of Frankenstein's Blood would drop to the floor in a dead faint to hear even a few words of a yet to be released song. "I'd love to."

He nodded and then strummed the strings, his voice ringing out husky and clear, and his eyes capturing hers and not letting go.

She was mine before I even knew she was mine...

A woman I can't live without

Though she might never be my own
A woman I can't stop thinking about
I wish she was mine alone
Because she was mine before I even knew she was mine...

Tiffany rubbed at her goose-bumped arms, sensing she'd heard the song before even though it'd yet to be recorded. And then it hit her. He'd sung it to her when she'd drifted off to sleep the night before!

Her own lullaby.

It was almost... incomprehensible. Women would sell their soul to be in her shoes right now. She put a hand to her mouth and listened in awe to his crooning voice, the emotion he injected into every word. It was breathtaking. Surreal.

He stopped playing and put his guitar back onto its stand. "You've inspired my muse."

She didn't know what to say to that. Instead, she quietly reveled in the moment, soaking it all in to examine more thoroughly another time.

Amos stepped toward her, his stare possessive, intense. "You probably realize now just how badly I want you." Emphasizing the point, he took her hand in his and pressed her palm against his erection.

She glanced up at him, her womb clenching and her sex moistening. "I'd say about as badly as I want you."

His stare glinted. "I'm no longer even sure I care about all the obstacles in our way. I just want to be with you."

She didn't have the willpower to tell him there was no happily ever after for them. But she'd always lived in the moment and, right now, she wanted him. She wouldn't—couldn't—think about a future without him in it.

He bent and kissed her, devoured her, and a hungry moan escaped her lips as he pulled her tight against him, mashing her belly to his bulging cock. Her arms slid around his neck like they truly belonged there, her fingers curling into the longish strands of his hair.

Their kiss deepened, their colliding bodies sending Tiffany stumbling back. Something tipped and crashed to the floor, something undoubtedly expensive. Amos whirled her away even as she dragged her mouth from his.

His eyes burned. "Don't worry about it." Then he lifted her and she wrapped her legs around his hips, their mouths joining once again as he strode out of the room and into a bedroom. Not that she took the time to notice.

All she comprehended was something soft beneath her spine before she toed off her boots and they feverishly helped one another out of their clothes.

She reclined, naked, back onto the bed and Amos followed her. It felt so right for him to lean down, his eyes blazing and his cock poised between her thighs. Felt all too acceptable when he growled, "No more condoms between us, okay?"

She nodded, knowing it wasn't acceptable behavior as a call girl but trusting Amos with everything she had, and all too aware this would be their last night together. "Okay," she answered huskily.

He slid into her with a hissed breath, his eyes barely focused, with pleasure clearly swamping over him. The pleasure was equally shared. Having his bare length sink balls-deep into her was incredible, her nerve endings tingling and alive, while every cell rejoiced even before he pumped fast and then faster inside her.

Her back arched and she lifted her legs. Amos' primal grin pushed heat through her pussy even before he stilled for the couple of seconds needed to clasp her thighs and elevate her legs up and over his shoulders.

He kneeled, the most intimate part of her open for his inspection. He tipped his head back and squeezed his eyes closed, and she knew he was fighting not to stroke a couple more times before exploding inside her.

Except she wanted him to lose control, wanted to see him stripped bare of everything but desire. She waited a few beats, her whole body suspended with exhilaration, flushed with need and damp with want. The moment his hips drove forward again she realized *she* was the one who wasn't going to last more than a few seconds.

The angle of his stroke hit a special place inside her and she fell apart on his next downward stroke, stiffening for a nanosecond before her every muscle dissolved into putty. Her vision blurred and all rational thought vanished as heat barreled through her and lit her up from within.

The next instant, her inner muscles locked. Amos' jaw clenched and he thrust deep before his whole body jerked, his eyes glazing and his throat constricting as his seed spilled into her again and again.

She was just as awed by his response to her, the way he lost himself to her the moment they joined. The way his whole body seemed to need hers, and vice versa. She stifled a surge of trepidation and dropped her legs back onto the mattress. Their chemistry and connection wasn't exactly ideal, given their call girl and client roles.

Yet satisfaction left her warm and deliciously drowsy, even as Amos gently disengaged and then lay beside her, an arm moving across her belly and his lips brushing her scalp.

"We really need to talk," he murmured.

"About?"

"Our future."

She sucked in a jagged breath. *Way to spoil a perfect moment!* She no longer wanted to think about anything beyond the present, no longer wanted to think about anything but the wonder of great sex with a skilled lover.

She lifted her head to meet his warm stare, aware she needed to be... brutal. "You'll have to talk to Maisey if you want to secure more time with me."

For a second, he stared at her with unblinking eyes. Then he jerked away from her as if scalded. "You know I never meant it from a professional standpoint, right?"

Bloody hell. He was going to force her to hurt him even more just so that she could save her own heart from bleeding dry.

She pushed a note of censure into her voice. "You seriously can't believe we can ever be a couple outside of what we have now?"

"Why the hell not?" He growled. "Do you love your career and all those strangers you fuck more than what I'm offering?"

She sat, and his eyes this once didn't leave her face to take in the sway of her breasts, her aroused and flushed, naked body. "Just what exactly *are* you offering?"

He pushed to his feet, pain and rage and a whole lot of other emotions stamped onto his face. "Me! Hell, my fortune too, if that's what you want!"

Something within her withered and died a little. God, she deserved that. She'd given him nothing but the woman who lived for sex and money. Yet she desperately wanted so much more than that, craved what he offered until it took everything she had not to crumble.

Her chin lifted. "I'm sorry, it wouldn't work."

Color drained from his face. His hands fisted, his knuckles going white. "Then tell me what I have to do to make you change your mind?"

Her heart beat double-time, her willpower sucked ever so slowly under by a rising tide of hope.

This time, it was her hands fisting as she croaked out, "You can meet my dad."

Chapter Nine

Amos couldn't keep his eyes off Tiffany as she climbed into the back of the limousine that waited just outside his Sydney home. The helicopter ride had been a rather silent affair, but he hadn't pressed her for more details about her father and why she wanted Amos to meet him.

It was clearly a big deal for her, one he wasn't going to make her regret.

He climbed in beside her. "I can have the driver take you home first if you'd prefer to freshen up and change?"

Not that she didn't look damn fine in jeans and a long-sleeved shirt, but whatever she felt most comfortable in was all he cared about. Besides which, he'd get to see where she lived.

She brushed a hand along her denim-clad thighs. "Thanks, but this is the perfect attire for seeing my dad."

He ignored a deep pang of disappointment and leaned back against the plush leather seat, his mind ticking over and his instincts coming to the fore. Either her father didn't know she was an escort or he couldn't accept it. Amos didn't doubt for a second there wouldn't be many parents who'd like the idea of their daughter being in the sex game.

He frowned. He knew so little about Tiffany, her family, her background. Jesus, he didn't even know her real name.

He turned to her. "What do I call you in front of your father?"

Her hands squeezed together in her lap and he had to ruthlessly quash a desire to pull her into his arms. He wanted answers from her, and he wanted them now. Touching her would only distract them.

She looked up at him. "My real name is Natalie."

"Natalie," he murmured, testing out her name and feeling honored to know it. "It suits you."

She huffed out a breath. "The name probably goes better with my jeans and cotton shirt."

He chuckled, a visual of Tiffany in her sexy lingerie and call girl outfits flashing through his head. His dick jerked in response. He'd gladly fuck Natalie in whatever guise she preferred, even though right now he'd happily settle for a long, drugging kiss. But he was pushing her boundaries just in meeting her father, she probably needed her space.

He cleared his throat. "Natalie is a girl next door kind of name." He ran the back of his knuckles along the silken skin of her jaw, giving in to his need to touch her. "It's perfect."

She blinked up at him, the blue of her eyes reminding him of the calmest ocean, but with a turbulent current beneath. "And do you prefer being with Tiffany or Natalie?" she asked.

He chose his words carefully. "Tiffany and Natalie is the same girl, just with different guises." He shrugged. "I guess what I'm trying to say is that I'm just as happy to rip off your jeans as I am a cocktail dress or lingerie."

She sighed, her tension easing. "I've never told a client my real name, not even Toby."

Amos gritted his teeth at the burning sensation in his chest. "Is Toby the client you fell in love with?"

She nodded, and then looked away. "Yes."

He cupped her chin and drew her back to face him. "You deserve better."

He wanted to tell her she deserved *him*. But, most of all, he wanted to tell her he needed her in his life permanently. He no longer kidded himself that freedom was important; he'd give that up in a heartbeat to have Natalie in his life. But not if she stayed an escort. It would slowly eat him alive knowing she was spending the night with a client while he lay alone in his big, empty bed.

First though, he had to make Jasmine understand he had zero feelings for anyone else but Natalie. Hell, he'd gladly pay Jasmine off, if it meant she'd give up on him and leave Natalie alone.

"Call girls and permanent relationships don't mix," she said quietly.

His thoughts exactly. "Would you consider giving up your profession?"

She looked away, and his hand dropped from her face when she said, "I'm not sure that's even possible. You'll soon... understand why."

"Nothing's impossible." Otherwise, she wouldn't have relented and asked him to meet her father.

The limousine slowed and pulled beside the curb of a concrete driveway, but he wasn't taking too much notice of the house, he was more interested in Natalie's reaction. With her lips pressed together and her hands clasped tightly in her lap, nervous energy fairly radiated from her.

If she was any stiffer, she'd shatter.

"Are you okay?" he asked gently.

She nodded and gave him a too quick smile, but, if anything, she looked paler. It was only once the chauffeur had opened the back door and Amos walked with her up the wide pathway and then a ramp to the front door, that he realized her father might well be disabled.

She pressed the front door buzzer, and he turned to her and asked, "Isn't he expecting us?" It seemed odd to him that a daughter would need permission to enter a parent's home.

Natalie shook her head. "He hates having visitors."

"I'm sorry he feels that way."

Then the door opened to a thickset man in a wheelchair, his thick shock of iron-gray hair matching his steely gray stare. His eyes only softened a fraction on seeing his daughter.

"Nat, what are you doing here?" he asked gruffly.

"It's good to see you too, Dad," she returned drily, bending then to kiss his leathery, whiskered cheek.

Amos watched the exchange with interest. The father-daughter dynamic might well be the key to Natalie's reluctance to leave her career as an escort and date him exclusively.

"You know I love seeing my daughter," her father said gruffly.

She arched a blonde brow. "You just don't like me seeing you."

He snorted. "I'm an invalid, a cripple; I don't want anyone seeing me like this. And I most especially don't want you to remember me like this when I'm gone."

Her head jerked back as though she'd been slapped. "You're still a warrior here," she choked out, pressing a hand to her heart.

Her father's eyes dampened, and he looked away from her with the kind of soul-decaying weariness Amos related to all too well. The older man's stare connected to him and Amos stepped closer to proffer his hand. "It's a privilege to meet you, sir."

When the older man didn't extend his own hand, and instead stared up at him with a curled lip and distrust clear in his stare, Natalie cleared her throat and said, "My goodness, where are my manners. Dad, this is Amos. Amos this is my dad, Stanley." She exhaled a panicked breath as she focused back on her father. "I've been seeing Amos recently and I thought it was time you met him."

Stanley barely looked at his daughter, not when all his attention was directed at Amos. "What are your intentions with my daughter?"

Amos had dealt with plenty of overzealous fans, both male and female, performed on stage to thousands who watched his every move and listened to his every note, but he'd never felt judged so badly. A lesser man might have squirmed.

"My intentions are honorable." He wouldn't mention paying Natalie for sex, that wouldn't look great for either one of them. "We're... dating.

Stanley stared harder, clearly not convinced. "Are you now?" He looked at Natalie then. "Well, then, no point standing outside the front door when I have a perfectly functional house to entertain in."

The older man spun the wheelchair around, his gnarly hands pushing on its wheels to lead the way inside. Amos followed Natalie, a part of him admiring the sway of her delectable butt in the jeans he'd bought her. Not to mention her topknot of hair that was still mussed from their quad bike adventure and bedroom fun.

His lips curled. Her hair suited her perfectly.

She looked wild, wicked, and wanton.

When his dick jerked with agreement, he stifled a curse. He only hoped the sharp-eyed Stanley wouldn't notice his predicament.

Stanley turned to them in a lounge and dining room combo that was separate from the kitchen. The house was clean and uncluttered, but with very few family pictures or signs of love. It was most definitely a house, not a home.

Stanley eyed them. "I'm guessing you've both eaten? If not, I was about to have some lunch if you'd like to join me?"

"Actually, that'd be great Dad," Natalie said with a smile that told Amos the invite didn't often happen.

"Kasey!" Stanley shouted into the hallway with cupped hands. "I've got visitors. They're staying for lunch." He turned to Amos then, his mouth pinched. "Don't you feed my daughter, then?"

Amos barely stifled a grin. The old man was really gunning for him. In a way he was glad. Natalie deserved a man who'd treat her like a princess; she was a woman worthy of way more than her present situation.

"Well?" Stanley gruffly demanded.

"Daddy, seriously?"

Amos curled an arm around Natalie's slender shoulders, and kissed the top of her head. "I had a picnic planned on a mountaintop cabin, but your daughter had other ideas, ones that involved visiting her father. I wasn't about to deny her that."

Stanley's suspicious stare glimmered with the smallest bit of respect. "You know how to say all the right things, I'll give you that."

Natalie giggled, her eyes shining as she glanced up at Amos. "I said the exact same thing." At Stanley's puzzlement, she added, "Amos is a singer-songwriter."

Her father's mouth slackened. "A musician?" He croaked, like the very word was toxic to his health. He pushed a hand over his face. "The sex, drugs, and rock n' roll type of musician?"

"I don't do drugs, and I steer clear of groupies." He wouldn't elaborate on why he kept away from groupies; that was one lesson he'd learned the hard way and would keep to himself. At least for now.

Stanley's harrumph was interrupted by the arrival of a portly, middle-aged woman who had to be Kasey. The dark-haired woman's smile lit up the room when she saw Natalie. She placed a teapot and a platter of sandwiches and cream biscuits onto the dining table before she enveloped Natalie in a hug.

"It's so good to see you here"—she turned to Amos—"and with a friend too."

It warmed Amos' heart to know it was rare for Natalie to bring anyone home, and most especially a male friend. It didn't bear thinking about that she was probably too busy making strangers every sexual dream come true instead.

Natalie introduced Amos to Kasey, who was Stanley's live-in carer. The whole mood lightened considerably with the other women there breaking the tension. They stayed for half an hour, chatting about inconsequential things while they ate a lunch of cold beef sandwiches with cheese, tomato, and pickles.

It was only when they were about to leave and Natalie leaned toward Kasey and quietly enquired about her dad's expenses, that it hit him. Holy shit! She was paying for all her father's medical bills. No longer was it hard to understand the whys of her being a call girl.

"If you need more for anything, just ask," Natalie added.

Kasey smiled and gave Natalie's hand a reassuring squeeze. "Of course."

When they were in the back of the limousine again and pulling away from her father's house, Amos watched Natalie's tension leech out. "I know a great way to release any lingering stiffness." He teased.

"Honestly, I think I just want a hot bubble bath and twelve hours of unbroken sleep."

He put a hand on her thigh and gave her a reassuring squeeze. "You're not working tonight."

He had one more night to try and convince her they belonged together.

She shook her head, shocked and yet tellingly relieved at his admission. "Do you have *any* money left in your bank account?"

He grinned. Did she have no idea of his true value? He could probably buy a small country with the money that poured in from his music. "I think Maisey is stressing that another of her call girls is going to leave. But I guess money was still a big enough motivator for her to juggle the agency's clients around."

"So you've seriously paid for my company again tonight?"

He nodded. "Yes, but it's your choice if you want my driver to drop you off at your home, or come back to my place."

She frowned and exhaled heavily, and he held his breath as he waited for her to reach a decision. When she subsided against him and said, "Your place is closer," he wasn't sure whether to be relieved or disappointed.

He wanted almost desperately to know her address. Because knowing it meant she trusted him in a way a girlfriend trusted a boyfriend. Hell, he wasn't asking for a front door key, not just yet, even though his entire being ached to be a part of her life.

She put her head on his shoulder and he rested his head on hers. He couldn't expect her to trust him when they knew so little about one another. Resolve steeled his shoulders and warmed his heart.

When Natalie woke tomorrow after a much needed sleep, he'd get past her defenses to learn more about her on a personal level. One this time that didn't involve taking off one another's clothes.

He'd save that pleasurable activity for another time.

Chapter Ten

Natalie stretched, enjoying Amos' cool silk sheets and his hot, powerful body snuggled against hers. She'd woken easily ten minutes earlier, but she'd wanted to stay asleep. She'd never felt safer or more secure, her body and soul in complete harmony.

Her cell phone buzzed and she whimpered. The sound was a disturbance she didn't want to register. It was the same sound that would forcibly bring her back into the real world where bills waited, along with clients.

"You'd better answer that," Amos said in a sleepy, amused voice next to her. "Whoever it is, isn't about to give up."

She cracked open an eye, and then reached for the phone she'd left on the side table next to Amos' big bed. Blinking groggily, she read caller ID. She jerked wide awake and sat with a sharp gasp, answering the call. "Toby?"

"Tiffany." For a moment she brushed aside a flare of annoyance that in all the months she'd known him, he hadn't once asked for her real name.

Instead, she cleared her throat and said, "Yes."

His voice quavered. "I need to see you."

Her heart skipped a beat. If he'd asked this from her just a few short days ago she would have jumped through hoops to see him again. Now she felt nothing more than mild curiosity and a stirring of resentment. "Whatever for?"

He exhaled sharply. "Christ, you really need to ask that?"

Her eyes narrowed. She'd been waiting for over three months to hear back from him. She would have been happy with a few warm words, some crumbs of affection from him, anything that would back up what he'd told her. But she'd heard nothing, and had assumed the worst.

She wasn't good enough. A hooker was only meant for some fun in the bedroom, not a lifelong commitment.

She twisted a little to view Amos. He was wide awake and watchful, but his hands behind his head in no way made him look relaxed. She sent him a weak smile before she turned away and concentrated on the man she'd actually believed she loved. "Actually, yes, I do."

His voice sounded hollowed out when he burst out with, "My wife signed the divorce papers."

She stiffened, every cell in her body going into high alert.

She rubbed at hand over her temple. "Are you for real?"

"Of course I am. Tiffany, what is going on? This is what you wanted, what we both wanted."

Not anymore it wasn't. But despite how Toby had treated her, she couldn't explain her change of heart toward him, not on the phone, and not without Amos hearing the truth.

She swallowed and squeezed her eyes shout. *I've fallen in love with Amos.*

She clutched the phone in her hands as Toby blabbered on in her ear. She really did love Amos; there was no denying it anymore. She softly sighed. She needed to tell Toby there was no hope between them, needed to tell him to patch things up with his wife or get on with his life alone.

"Look, I can't talk to you right now." She cut in. "Meet me at the Crazy Duke Inn in an hour and we'll talk there."

She disconnected the call and turned again to face Amos.

"You're really going back to him," he said in a flat voice.

She frowned. "I didn't say that."

"But you still love him."

She gaped. "No! Of course I don't."

His eyes darkened. "You fell in love with a married man, sounds to me like he's a free agent now."

So he'd overheard at least some of Toby's conversation. It was odd how deep Amos' distrust cut.

She pushed out of bed and scooped up her clothes, reverting to her career choice to cover her pain. "I'm a call girl. I'm not sure you should be too bothered about an ex-client of mine."

She pulled on her underwear, jeans, and top he'd flown in for her, trying not to dwell on the fact no other man had even done anything halfway as special for her. Clients wanted sex, not to please their escort. But, from the very start, Amos had been different. Special.

She bloody adored him.

But her emotions were too new, too raw to wrap her head around right then. Especially with this latest piece of news stirring things up.

Amos sat, his face grim with purpose. "Natalie, don't go. Please. Not until we talk."

She crossed her arms, defiance and hurt and whole lot of other mixed-up emotions swirling in her gut. "Okay, then talk."

He frowned, clearly not liking the way their conversation had started. "I want to take our... relationship to the next level. But to do that we need to learn more about one another. We need to open up."

Her heart jolted and then warmed, her senses sharpening. She was hopeful and scared all at the same time, because opening up meant trusting one another. Opening up also meant being exposed with the possibility of out-and-out failure.

She nodded, but her voice cracked with tension. "All right. You first."

He raked a hand through his hair. "I've never been great at relationships. Hell, I've never even really had one." His voice quieted.

"Not when love and abandonment has always seemed intrinsically linked."

"You're speaking from experience." It wasn't a question, not when his openness betrayed a past hurt that couldn't be concealed.

"Yes." He didn't look away; instead, he seemed desperate for her to read him, to understand him. "My parents died in a car accident when I was sixteen." He exhaled heavily. "I was the driver."

She pressed a shaky hand to her mouth. "I'm so sorry."

He shook his head. "Don't be sorry, not for me. I don't deserve it. I was the one who took the turn too fast. I was also the one who caused the car to roll and hit a tree." He blinked, his face going pale. "My dad was in the front passenger seat, he died from the impact. My mom would have been fine... if she'd been able to unclip her seatbelt."

Natalie climbed onto the bed and pulled him against her, stroking his head even as he continued, his voice breaking. "The tree was splintering under the car's weight, and it began to slip down the incline that led to a cliff and the ocean below. There was no time to do anything but try and free my mother from her seatbelt."

She gripped him harder, loving him so much it hurt. She only wished she could take away even some of his pain.

"The car lurched and the tree literally groaned, as though telling us it couldn't hold the car back much longer. Mom grabbed my hand as if in goodbye, and then she told me to get out, that she didn't want me to die too." He sucked in a breath. "She was crying when she told me she loved me, and that she and dad would always watch over me." He swallowed audibly. "I'll never forget her tears."

Natalie didn't say anything, she simply held him fast. No words could take away the memory that was no doubt as sharp in his head now as it was all those years ago.

"When I refused, she begged me to get out." He swallowed audibly. "I ignored her and reached for her seatbelt. But then the tree trunk cracked and the car slipped free. I think... I think it was as much self-preservation as any sort of obedience when I shoved open my door and rolled free."

She pulled back, and then kissed him gently, first his mouth and then the bead of a tear that slipped down his cheek. "You were incredibly brave and strong." She held his stare. "You did everything in your power to free your mother. Everything. No one would ever dispute that. Not your mother or your father."

"If I hadn't been driving, they might still be alive today."

"They might be," she said softly. "Except accidents happen every single day of the week, where people are taken from their children, their families. It's harsh but it's the truth. Anyone could have been driving that car, with the same results. Call it fate. Call it horrible timing. Call it whatever you want, but it's *not* your fault."

He kissed her back then, his lips soft and yet tender, his emotions bared to her. When he finally pulled back, he said huskily, "Thank you. I've been carrying that around for a long time. I'm glad I could share it with you."

She cupped his strong jaw, with its coarse growth of bristles. Dear Lord, hadn't he told anyone else? Somehow, she knew he hadn't, not for a very long time, probably not since the police had questioned him about the accident. She only hoped a counselor had been involved along the way.

"Are the tattoos on your back a reminder of them?"

He nodded. "Yeah. My mother loved red shoes and couldn't resist buying them. The white roses are what my father bought my mom every payday without fail, no matter how much they struggled to pay their bills. Everyone brought white roses to the funeral in honor of their love."

Her breath hitched at the raw pain in his voice, but she refused to change the subject to avoid further stress. She sensed he was glad to share his past as much as she wanted to hear it. She ran a hand down his back, wishing she could feel the ink like braille. "And the script underneath?"

He pushed his head against her other hand, as though needing her close. "Mom and Dad, May Your Love be Forever Entwined." His smile was etched with sadness. "Dad taught Latin at the local college, so I had it inked in that language."

Her chest ached for him but she still managed a smile. "I'm glad you trusted me enough to share it with me."

His eyes glittered. "Natalie, I love you."

She sucked in a breath, her heart expanding. "I love you too," she said huskily.

Why had it taken her so long to realize he was truly the only man for her? Why hadn't she comprehended that nothing in life was impossible, not even a client falling in love with her?

Good things didn't just happen to women like Brandy and Scarlet, they happened to her too. She too deserved a man like Amos, deserved to be loved and cherished. If only life didn't sometimes make a person feel unworthy of it.

She bit into her bottom lip, her eyes closing. What happened if Amos *did* hurt her? She'd left herself open now, vulnerable to hurt.

"Don't shut me out, Natalie. Open your eyes. Let me in."

She released a slow breath and did as he asked, giving herself over to him completely. She couldn't spend her whole life shielding herself from possible hurt. She needed to grab Amos, by the throat if need be, and trust in him and his word.

He stared at her with unblinking eyes. "I really do love you."

Her heart did a slow somersault. She was a fool to think she could deny what had blossomed between them. "And I really do love you too," she whispered.

A slow smile spread over his face, his eyes bright with adoration. "Come on tour with me."

Her thoughts scattered like leaves in the wind. "What?"

"We leave tonight for a tour around Australia before we hit Asia and the US." He blinked. "Say you'll come with me and leave your old life behind." He brushed some strands of loose hair behind her ear. "I'll take care of everything. All your expenses, Maisey… everything."

Mirth bubbled up inside her, a barely withheld release of tension and control. "I've never told you this before, but I'm a huge fan of Frankenstein's Blood."

His grin wavered, his head tipping to the side. "You are?"

She nodded. "Yes. I just didn't want you to know it. Didn't want you to imagine I was just another groupie ready to kiss your damn feet."

His eyes flashed with an odd light, but then his smile returned full force and he murmured, "So that's a yes, then?"

She bit into her bottom lip. "My father—"

"Will have his every need met, I'll make sure of it."

Any doubts evaporated as warmth radiated through her, her trilling laugh finally escaping before she burst out, "Yes!" and flung herself into his arms.

When their mouths met in a kiss that deepened in urgency and need, the last thing on her mind was being late meeting Toby. All she cared about was the man whose arms held her as if he'd never let her go.

Even before he undressed her with practiced hands, kissing her bared, sensitized skin until she was quivering and moaning beneath him, then pushed inside her, making her gasp with the pleasure-pain of joining, she knew without a doubt she'd already given him her heart, her soul.

There was no going back from that.

Chapter Eleven

Natalie walked into the Crazy Duke Inn with a weight off her shoulders and lightness in her step. She grinned. Here she was, a twenty-seven-year-old woman, happy for the first time since her mother had walked out of the family home fifteen years ago.

It was heady, to say the least, knowing Amos loved her with everything he had. Knowing he now waited for her to return and join him at his house, where they'd then leave together for his national and then international tour was simply the icing on the cake.

She'd always wanted to see Australia and the rest of the world, but had always thought it was a pipe dream. Now it was as if her whole future was spread out before her like a glorious fantasy just waiting to come true.

She put a hand to her mouth. Who'd have thought her jaw could ache and her whole face hurt from smiling so much? Not she was complaining, not when her whole body felt truly alive.

Heading toward the bar, it was hard to miss Toby's broad back in his dark business suit, and his silver hair that appeared to have thinned even more.

He sensed her approach, his head turning and his gray eyes lighting up when he saw her. "Tiffany, finally. I was starting to think you'd blown me off."

She almost winced at him using her call girl name. But she'd accept being Tiffany one last time, before leaving that part of her life far behind her. Besides, it wasn't as if she wanted Toby to learn her real name.

He retrieved a glass of wine from the bar. "I ordered your favorite shiraz," he said with a smile, before they walked over to a more private area in a corner of the room.

She refrained from telling him that gin and tonic was now her drink of choice, but she had more important things to get off her chest first. Not that she'd be here long. She'd even left her clutch bag in the chauffeured car as she didn't expect this reunion would last much longer than a few minutes.

He pulled out a seat for her in a show of gentlemanly intent, and she bit back a sigh of exasperation. It was all too little too late, she'd fallen for a man worthy of her now.

He sat opposite her. "Tiffany, I'm sorry I didn't get in touch with you before now, you must think me a real cad."

She took a big sip of her drink, trying not to laugh. Who even used the word "cad" these days?

"How is your wife?" she asked instead.

"Ex-wife." He hurriedly corrected. His hand tightened on his glass. "She's been better, I'd imagine. It wasn't easy for her to find out I'd been having sex with the same call girl over a period of several months."

She bristled. So, was Toby's wife more upset their "relationship" had been longer than a one-night stand, or by the fact he'd paid for sex? She wiped a bead of condensation from her glass. "Did you tell her we haven't seen one another for some time now?"

It'd been over three months since Toby had professed his undying devotion to Tiffany and promised to leave his wife. Of course she hadn't heard anything from him since... until now.

He frowned. "Of course, but she won't listen to me. She was furious, distraught. I betrayed her in the worst possible way."

So confessing his love to Tiffany and then abandoning her for all those months wasn't a betrayal? She pushed away the disparaging thought. It hardly mattered to her what Toby did anymore; she felt disconnected to him now. She was only glad a decent, honorable man like Amos had opened her eyes.

She focused on the dishonorable man in front of her. God, what had she even seen in him? He'd even been selfish in bed, but she'd excused it by imagining all men were the same.

She cleared her throat. "Do you still love her?"

He gulped down some of his beer. "I'd love her a lot more if she'd give out once in a while." He sighed. "But, honestly, I don't fantasize about her like I do you, and I most certainly don't want to fuck her like I want to fuck you."

She stifled a frown. Maybe his wife—ex-wife—didn't want to have sex with Toby because he didn't show her any passion.

His eyes gleamed as they roamed over Tiffany's everyday look of jeans and a shirt. Somehow, she felt more exposed than she ever had in her lingerie and sexy call girl outfits. Somehow, she felt anything other than sexy. She felt soiled... used.

As if sensing her mental distance, Toby's shoulders slumped. He sighed dejectedly. "Whatever I once felt for my wife just isn't there anymore. She's a friend, nothing more."

Unwitting sympathy filled her for Toby's wife. The fact Tiffany had been paid to sleep with such a callous man left a bitter taste in her mouth. It also cemented the fact she was no longer cut out for the life of a call girl. *Who* her client was shouldn't matter, only the size of their wallets.

But it was enlightening to finally uncover the truth. She'd happily leave her professional life behind to embrace a life with Amos. She'd also happily make love with Amos for the rest of her life and never again have to service another stranger.

Ever.

"Well, isn't this a lovely surprise."

Tiffany turned at the same time as Toby to view the dark-haired lady stalking toward them, the same woman who'd given off strange vibes in the underground cabaret club.

"I'm sorry," Tiffany said, "I saw you talking to Amos, but we haven't officially met."

The woman stilled before them, her eyes flashing. "Of course we haven't officially met. Why would Amos want to introduce his girlfriend to his whore?"

Tiffany's joy dissipated faster than smoke in the wind. But she couldn't believe it, not when Amos had looked her in the eye and told her there was no other woman waiting for him at home. "You're lying."

"Oh, please, why would I lie?" She held up her cell phone to show her the text message from Amos.

Tiffany felt something die a little inside when she read the message. *"Jasmine, I need to see you urgently. When can we meet?"*

The message had been sent just minutes after she'd left Amos to meet Toby. Her throat thickened, trapping her breath. Oh, god. Amos hadn't even waited ten minutes before wanting to see another woman.

Jasmine shrugged. "Of course, he hasn't yet committed to marriage; he's too busy sowing his wild oats. But I'm a realist. He's a potent sexual male and, while he's on tour, he won't refuse a beautiful woman in his bed."

Natalie couldn't think, could barely even focus on the woman who was filling her mind with poison. She pressed a fist to her churning belly. Dear God, had Amos seriously planned on taking Tiffany on tour to fulfill his sexual needs, before dumping her for Jasmine the minute he returned home?

She was numb, yet she automatically assessed the other woman in the hope to find her lacking. Only to decide Jasmine was a respectable woman who'd probably only had a couple of steady boyfriends in her life.

Jasmine was perfect wife material.

Toby watched Jasmine with a frown marring his already craggy face. "I have no idea who you are, but rest assured you no longer have anything to worry about with your boyfriend. Tiffany is with me now."

A slow burn rose in Natalie's face, until she finally snapped, "No, Toby, I'm *not* with you. I'll never be with you! I don't trust you. In fact, I don't trust any man! I'd suggest you go back to you poor, suffering wife and beg her for forgiveness. Not that you deserve her."

She turned to Jasmine next, ignoring the woman's snide little smile to add through gritted teeth, "Tell Amos I hope he has a wonderful orgy while he's on tour. And a wonderfully boring married life when he returns."

With that, she strode out of the hotel, not even trying to hold back scalding tears. The fact she no longer gave a stuff about Toby might have been a bigger relief if Amos' betrayal didn't stab her in the heart a thousand times worse. She should have listened to her instincts, should have ignored her traitorous heart and gotten on with her life without Amos in it.

She should have damn well known better!

The chauffeured car waited for her a little further up the road. She turned and strode the opposite direction. She needed to clear her head, needed to walk and walk until she couldn't walk any further.

She ignored the thickening crowd of pedestrians who sent her odd looks. But mostly people left her alone and minded their own business. She should probably be glad she wasn't in the country, where people usually cared enough to ask questions.

The blaring horn of a sedan startled her back off the road and onto the pavement. *Shit*. She swiped at her tears and sucked in a steadying breath, her pounding heart settling into a normal rhythm. She'd been steeped so deep in her own misery she'd been walking on autopilot, using the barest of her senses.

It was more of a surprise she hadn't already been hit by a car.

She dragged a hand over her face before glancing around and forcing herself to take note of her surroundings. She recognized the buildings and the intersection. If nothing else, at least she'd gone the right direction. It was less than a ten minute walk to her apartment. And although she'd left her bag with all her essentials in Amos' chauffeured car, at least she'd had the foresight to give her neighbor a spare key.

She patted her jeans pocket. And at least she still had her cell phone. She smiled grimly. An escort never went anywhere without their phone, for obvious reasons. Not that it made her feel any better about the situation.

By tomorrow, Amos would be long gone on his tour. She released a shaky breath. She only hoped she hadn't completely misjudged him and that he'd return her personal effects via the agency.

Though she wanted nothing more than to climb into bed and stay there until her tears had ran dry, she had no other choice but to get on with her life. She'd indulge in a shower and force down something to eat. Then she'd ring Maisey and make the necessary arrangements to meet her next client.

Her heart shriveled and her belly spun sickly. How quickly things could change in the space of a few minutes. No longer was she dreaming about leaving behind her call girl life and having no one else in her bed other than Amos, she was resuming a life of paying the next round of medical bills.

To do anything else would see her curling into a ball and never getting up again, and she wouldn't give into that temptation. Not for a cheating man who didn't deserve the heartbreak.

She lifted her chin. Amos could go find himself another "whore" to satisfy his wild oats, because she no longer wanted him in her life. He didn't need her. Not when he already had a woman waiting for him at his convenience.

The pedestrian light turned green and she strode across the road. The only thing she could do now was to get on with her life, take each day as it came. And hope to God the heavy ache in her chest would dull over time.

Chapter Twelve

Amos locked his Mustang and strode across the road. Although the pressure across his temple tightened at the coming confrontation with Jasmine, there was a spring in his step and lightness in his chest knowing he'd soon be with Natalie again.

He grinned. Soon have a future that featured Natalie in it.

As much as he was desperate to get rid of Jasmine and her obsession of him, he'd come to at least sympathize with those same deep, stark emotions. What he felt for Natalie must be dangerously close to what Jasmine felt for him. Except he was lucky the blonde bombshell returned his feelings in full.

He slowed as the outdoor tables and chairs of the eatery came into view. Jasmine had her back to him, but she soon stiffened and then turned, her eyes meeting his.

His grin faded as impatience hit him front and center. He had absolutely no feelings for Jasmine beyond a deep frustration that it'd come to this. He only wished she'd focus on chasing a man who wanted her in his bed and in his life.

He sat opposite her, trying not to dwell on the fact the Crazy Duke Inn was just a couple of blocks away. Trying not to imagine what Natalie and her ex-client Toby were discussing. He inhaled carefully. He definitely wouldn't rehash how Natalie had professed to once loving the man.

Jasmine smiled, a gleam of satisfaction in her stare immediately tensing the muscles across his shoulders and knotting his belly.

He forced a smile in return and clipped out, “Thanks for agreeing to see me so soon.”

She shrugged idly, her heart-shaped bodice half-exposing the jiggling, upper globes of her breasts. “You must know by now I’d do anything for you.”

What about leaving me the hell alone?

Amos kept his thoughts to himself and his attention above her neckline. Not because Jasmine’s obvious ploys to charm him worked, quite the contrary.

Even in her sexiest escort outfits, Natalie had displayed an effortless style and grace that caught his attention and aroused him without even trying.

He exhaled heavily. “And you must know your fixation with me has to stop.”

Her eyes flashed. “Is that what you came here to tell me?” Her voice rose. “Don’t you find me attractive, is that it?”

He frowned. “You’re a beautiful woman, I’m sure you know that. But looks aren’t the only quality I want in a woman.”

She leaned forward, resting her elbows on the table and her chin on her interlinked hands. “The sex we shared was incredible,” she said huskily, “you can’t deny that.”

His frown deepened. He could hardly even recall their one time together; the sex surely couldn’t have been that amazing? “It was purely a physical release. You know as well as I there was no emotional connection.”

Her fingers whitened, her voice sharpening. “Keep telling yourself that and you might even start to believe it.”

Anger flared and then subsided. He had no idea how he’d react if Natalie shunned him either. Not only that, he doubted he’d ever be able to give her up, he’d chase her to the ends of the earth if that was what it took.

Jesus, maybe he and Jasmine weren’t all that different at all.

Then the dark-haired woman blinked back sudden tears. His lips pinched. He wasn't falling for her wet eyes and trembling chin. She was a woman scorned and a consummate actress to boot. She'd already tried every trick in the book to get what she wanted.

What exactly *did* she really want from him? Evidently, it was a man whose heart belonged to another woman. His jaw clenched, his throat closing up as frustration expanded. He'd been so wrong, he wasn't anything like Jasmine. He could never stand by and watch Natalie sleep with other men.

He sighed. Why hadn't he realized Jasmine didn't care about love? She wanted the status symbol, a celebrated and wealthy boyfriend.

She wanted a trophy lover.

He pushed a hand over his face, feeling suddenly old. "Jasmine, I can tell you one thing right now, we'll never share a bed again." At her narrow-eyed, vindictive gaze, he added, "But what I *can* offer you is a payoff."

Her eyes sharpened, brightened, and she made a half-hearted attempted to thread scorn through her denial. "If you think I'm another one of your whores, you can think again—"

"Two hundred thousand to stay away from me and never contact me again." He smiled, but felt nothing but coldness. "And, more importantly, to stay away from Natalie."

Jasmine slumped back in her seat, her face pale and her expression almost resigned. Except he couldn't fail to notice the glitter of avarice in her stare even when she said, "Natalie... so that's her real name."

He ignored her question. "You will also receive a further fifty thousand if you decide to move to another city and start again." He flicked a look at his watch. "You have one minute to agree. Say the word and my lawyer will be here within the next two minutes with all the appropriate paperwork for you to sign."

He'd had this whole scenario organized even before Jasmine had texted back an address of where to meet. Having Natalie in his life was all he cared about anymore, and paying off the dark-haired witch was a small price to pay towards achieving that goal.

He swept Jasmine a look. She didn't look anywhere near as beautiful with her feverish, over-bright eyes and flushed skin. Greed was stamped all over her face. And although it made a nice change from her obsession, he was even gladder he hadn't been foolish enough to give in and stay with her. "Either way, once the minute is up I'm leaving here and you'll never see me again."

She bit into her bottom lip, indecision and yearning chasing over her face. Maybe some of those feelings had been real for him after all, he conceded. But in the end money would win out.

Her chair scraped back loudly and she pushed to her feet. "All right, I'll do it."

He stood with a grim smile of satisfaction and murmured, "Good choice. Your time was almost up."

He turned and nodded to the suited lawyer standing across the street waiting for the verdict. The lawyer would explain every facet of the paperwork to Jasmine. Explain what would happen if she broke the deal. Turning back to her, he rasped, "I'm sorry things didn't turn out quite the way you hoped."

She flushed, her eyes glittering. "Not as sorry as I am."

He nodded, and then turned on his heel to make his escape.

But not before she added, "But things might not turn out quite the way you hoped either."

He didn't turn back and ask exactly what she meant. He didn't want to play any more mind games with a woman he wanted out of his life. He checked the street for a break in the traffic before he strode toward his cherry red Mustang.

He had a little detour to make. He fired up the engine and pulled out onto the road. And though he told himself it was to make sure Natalie was fine, he knew it was as much to reassure himself.

When a few minutes later he cruised past the stretch limousine that was parked just down the road from the Crazy Duke Inn, he found the nearest available space on the curb to park before he strode to his limousine and it's driver, Joe.

Thin as a beanpole, Joe was standing outside the car, clearly waiting for his passenger.

"Natalie not back yet?" he asked Joe, his words clipped. He had no time for pleasantries, not when a bad feeling was tripping off his internal alarm.

Joe shook his head. "Not yet, sir."

Amos struggled to catch his breath. Fuck. Was it his turn for a panic attack after all these years of calm?

"Sir, are you okay?"

Amos forced a nod. "Is she still inside the inn?"

Joe's face paled a little, fully aware of his boss' frazzled state. "I haven't been inside. But I doubt she'd gone anywhere else."

"Why is that?"

Joe swept a hand to the back of the car. "She left her bag with me. No woman I know would ever willingly leave one of their most personal possessions behind."

"Yeah, except she's not like other women." He gritted out, before stalking to the Crazy Duke Inn and scanning the one level layout. There were probably twenty or thirty people inside, but there was no sign of his woman.

He turned, his gaze landing on a man sitting in the corner of the Inn, staring gloomily into his beer with an empty wine glass opposite him.

In three long strides, Amos was in front of the man. "Toby, is it?" he asked.

The other man looked up. A good-looking, Richard Gere type, with thinning gray hair and a deceitful air. "Yeah, do I know you?"

"No, you don't. But I believe we might share a common interest."

The other man frowned, before the truth dawned. "Tiffany," he said.

Amos couldn't help but chuckle darkly. "Is that what you call her? I use her real name."

Toby glowered. "She told you her real name?"

He nodded. "I can hardly call my future fiancée by her working name, can I?"

Toby pushed to his feet. "You're fucking marrying her?"

"If she'll have me, yes, I am."

A vein in Toby's temple throbbed into life, his eyes jagged with disbelief and more than a little envy. "That's bullshit. You know she's in love with me, right?"

The older man was lying, it was written all over his face. Natalie might have been a call girl, past tense, but Amos trusted her implicitly. Her profession might be built around lies to suit her particular client's tastes but, under her stunning surface, she was the girl next door.

"I hate to break it to you," Amos said with a casualness he was far from feeling, "but she feels nothing for you but contempt and distrust. You left her hanging high and dry, and I was the one who set her free."

Toby slowly sat back down. But it was evident he hadn't yet given up the fight when he looked up with flashing eyes and said, "Really? Is that why your little floozy spouted off to Tiffany about waiting to marry you after the tour?"

His heart twisted. "My little floozy?" He stabbed his fingers through his hair. "I'm guessing you're talking about Jasmine."

"Yes, I had a lovely chat to her after Tiffany stormed off. Jasmine's quite a woman. Might even take her up on the offer and meet up."

Amos curled his lip, feeling a deep distaste for the greasy worm who'd thrown away the best thing that could've happened to him. "Do what you want, Jasmine's a free agent."

Toby raised a brow and sucked down some more of his beer. "So you really have fallen for Tiff," he murmured.

"What man in his right mind wouldn't?" Before Toby had a chance to respond, Amos added neutrally, "Did Tiffany believe Jasmine?"

Toby laughed, his eyes alight with mirth. "Of course, she bloody did. She's a whore, men don't marry whores. They marry women like Jasmine."

Amos wasn't a violent man. But his whole body tensed, heat rushing through his body and sending his heart pounding. His fist flew, the bone jarring punch sending Toby sprawling from his chair and onto the floor.

Amos stood over him, his vision shot with red. "A man would be fortunate to find a woman who is truly beautiful inside and out."

A crowd of spectators was already drawing around them. He heard their excited whispers as recognition dawned. He scraped together his sanity and pulled his fist back to his side. This wasn't the kind of publicity he wanted or needed, but he'd do it all again in a heartbeat.

Toby sat with a groan, swiping the back of his hand across his bloodied nose before looking up at Amos with hatred leaking from his eyes. But he was smart enough to keep his mouth shut and his profanities to himself.

Amos' grin was a hard twitch of his lips. "Enjoy your lonely life." He spun on his heel and stalked away from the scene.

He didn't give a damn about the consequences of his actions. He didn't even give a damn about his tour.

All he cared about right then was the woman he needed to track down.

Dragging out his phone, he rang the VIP Desire Agency. Maisey answered on the first ring, and he said gruffly, "Hi, it's Amos. You're probably sick of hearing my voice, but I really need to see Tiffany."

He wouldn't let on to Maisey that he'd learned Tiffany's real name.

"Amos." She purred. "I never get sick of hearing your voice, not when it involves you purchasing more time with my girls. Speaking of which, the beautiful Savannah has had a late cancellation—"

"I'm not interested in anyone else. Just Tiffany."

"Well I'm sorry to hear that, but Tiffany has put in a request for a new client."

"She's what?" He heard his voice from a great distance away, his heart beating erratically in his chest and his blood pressure bubbling in his ears.

"I'm sorry, Amos, I know how much you like her. But my girls are my priority and I take their likes and dislikes into consideration." Her voice dropped. "Please tell me you didn't hurt her?"

He blew out a harsh breath, bristling with defense. "I wouldn't hurt a hair on her head."

"That's good to hear." Maisey's voice softened fractionally. "Please ring me any time if you have a change of heart and desire time alone with one of my other gorgeous girls."

Maisey disconnected the call and he resisted throwing his cell to the ground and stamping it underfoot. Instead, icy calm moved over him.

He had much to do.

Chapter Thirteen

Tiffany kept a smile pasted on her face as Harry escorted her around the crowded, grand opening of his latest Heavy-Weight fitness center. It was apparently his biggest center yet, an exclusive club where only the wealthiest clientele could afford membership.

It wasn't hard to believe. The place was beyond impressive, all multi-leveled chrome and glass. Squash courts, aerobic classes, martial arts, three gyms, and a heated pool where he'd hired a world-renowned coach to drill slobs into athletes—Harry's words—were just some of its attributes.

A fruit smoothie kiosk competed with a bar, where waiters circulated with trays of beers and champagne for the thirsty people wandering around and taking everything in. Two slender women in gold bikinis and sashes with the fitness center name written in bold handed out flyers and discount cards.

"This is going well," Harry said with a self-satisfied grin, putting his arm around Tiffany's shoulders before he brushed a kiss against her cheek. "I can't wait to celebrate its success later tonight," he murmured intimately.

She managed a smile but wondered if it was more a grimace. Her heart wasn't in it at all. Not even her client's decent looks and affable personality put a positive spin on the evening.

"You look gorgeous, by the way," Harry added, as though aware she needed encouragement.

She glanced down at her silver, sparkly, form-fitting dress with its thigh side-split and plunging neckline that showed off a generous amount of her cleavage. Her breasts had been the perfect fit for Amos' big, callused hands.

She shivered, her nipples hardening and her womb clenching. Maybe she could get through tonight by closing her eyes and imagining Harry was Amos?

Harry's voice deepened. "I see you're looking forward to it too." His hand tightened around her shoulders and his fingers grazed her upper arm. A pity she experienced no answering response. She felt empty, disaffected. Numb.

Harry didn't seem to notice, and Tiffany couldn't help but judge. Amos had observed her every nuance of expression, had sensed her every mood. Her jaw tightened. It was probably an acquired skill he'd picked up from all the women he'd seduced.

She frowned. She had no doubt he'd make Jasmine a very happy wife one day.

A reporter approached with a clack of high heels and Harry's arm tightened possessively around Tiffany, before he introduced her as his "date".

The slender reporter, with her sleek auburn bun and long-lashed eyes, assessed Tiffany with a speculative gaze. "So, you're no longer with Amos, from Frankenstein's Blood?"

Tiffany's belly squeezed tight at the reminder. Had word gotten around that fast? Obviously, just being seen with Amos was newsworthy.

She put on a calm face and said politely, "No, Amos has moved on."

The reporter arched a brow and scribbled into a notepad. "That's interesting. Gossip has it that he was smitten."

"Who wouldn't be?" Harry interjected smoothly, before he steered the conversation in the direction of his grand opening.

The reporter looked annoyed, but got on with her job, while Tiffany nodded and smiled at the appropriate moments. But all the while, her thoughts strayed to Amos. Did he have any clue that Jasmine had told her the truth? When had he realized she wasn't coming back? Was he even now at his concert, maybe even planning to sing the song he'd written for her?

She sighed, hating she wanted to know that and so much more. Hated that she still wanted to be with him, despite the fact he'd planned to get rid of her the moment he settled down after his world tour.

What if you'd been able to change his mind in those months on tour? What if he decided he couldn't live without you, after all?

She shoved away the thought with ruthless determination. She'd once thought she'd loved Toby too and she'd been wrong. She should have learned her lesson the first time around. Except, while her feelings for Amos had been deep and real, whatever she'd felt for Toby had been shallow at best.

"Fitness and health is the mainstay of my life, the key to looking amazing." Tiffany zoned back into the one-sided conversation between Harry and the reporter, and smiled at the jaded woman jotting down pertinent notes.

Harry needed Tiffany to look gorgeous on his arm, since it gave his brand and his image a nice boost. Working out attributed to a person looking good. She hid a sudden smile. She wasn't about to let on that her exercise routine entailed nothing more than sexual workouts with her many clients.

The reporter scribbled down the last of her notes and took a photo of them, before Harry led Tiffany toward comfy lounges and square tables in a quieter corner of the room. They sat on a two-seater, and Harry lifted a hand and motioned over a waiter.

Taking two champagne flutes, he passed one to Tiffany and then raised his glass. "To a successful launch and an amazing night ahead."

She downed the fizzy champagne in just a couple of gulps. She'd need all the courage she could get. She fought back a rising tide of hysteria. No call girl she knew dreaded a night with a handsome, half-decent man. And lord only knew she'd been with a lot worse clients than Harry.

Clients like Toby, who promised the world and gave her nothing.

Meeting Amos, falling in love with him... it'd wrecked everything for her. She wasn't just crying inside, she was bleeding, her heart ripped into little pieces.

Harry moved closer, his eyes glinting. He had no idea she was slowly dying inside. He took her glass and put it onto a low table with his own glass. When he turned back to her, he said huskily, "I don't know how I'm going to last the night without fucking you right here, right now."

He clasped the back of her head, before he bent and kissed her. She put her hands on his shoulders, but not to revel in the wet kiss. God help her, she wanted only to shove him away, and then run and never look back.

"Natalie."

She stiffened. It was the one name guaranteed to get her attention. That it was Amos who spoke it had all her synapses to snapping to attention even before she turned to drink in the man she wanted with every damn fiber of her being.

Harry jerked back, his face flushed and his stare flashing. "What the hell are you doing here? Don't you have a concert or something to perform?"

She blinked, distantly aware that what Harry said was true. Amos was meant to be on tour. But, instead, he was here, staring at her as though she was the last woman on the planet.

She swallowed past her suddenly dry throat. He held her clutch bag, with Harry's business card in hand. At least she knew how he'd tracked her down. Except, even holding her dainty bag, he looked every inch a primal warrior, a man that Harry and every gym junkie in the building would want to emulate.

His forearms bulged in his black t-shirt, his legs long and strong in custom-ripped jeans. But it was his hard stare and his *take no prisoners* expression that caused her breath to catch in her throat and butterflies to flutter deep in her belly.

"I'm here to take my woman home," Amos announced. "The tour can wait."

Her throat constricted. He sounded like a caveman, like Tarzan. Add in his absolute certainty that she belonged to him and no one else, not to mention that she was more important than his concert; his fans, and damned if her willpower didn't melt away faster than snow meeting lava.

Harry eyed Amos with disbelief. "I paid for her. For tonight, at least, she's mine."

Amos' jaw tightened. "Like hell." He looked stronger, taller in his conviction.

Tiffany—or was she Natalie now—watched the drama unfold like she was a spectator in her own dream. She pressed a shaky hand to her mouth, resisting a sudden desire to wipe away the taste of Harry's lips.

Her hand dropped and she lifted her chin in challenge. "Amos, I'm not your woman."

Something flickered in Amos' stare, something that looked like pain. Her heart hardened. He'd probably never once experienced rejection before.

His tone was resolute, strong. "I'm not leaving without you. You're more than my woman; you're my heart and soul. You're my fucking everything."

She almost caved... almost. Except she was no longer the same naïve call girl who'd fallen for him hook, line, and sinker. She wasn't the same woman who'd handed him her heart on a silver platter. Nowhere near it.

Harry turned back to her, his mouth a tight line and his eyes full of questions. "Is this why you can't be with him, because he's in love with you?"

"No." Her voice cracked. "Amos can't be my client because I'm in love with him."

Amos inhaled sharply. "You are?"

Hadn't he believed her the first time? Her eyes burned with pain and unshed tears. "My feelings don't turn on and off like a switch."

Harry shook his head, now more bemused than upset. "Tiffany, if you really want to be with him... then be with him."

Amos stepped forward. "I *know* Natalie wants to be with me. Which is why she can't be with you tonight. She can't be with anymore clients."

Harry raised a brow. "Except I've already paid for her services."

"I'll pay you ten times what you paid the agency."

Natalie felt frozen in the spot. Not because of the crowd gathering around—most notably the fascinated reporter who scribbled down all the juicy details—but because she was once again drowning in yearning and hope. Drowning in emotions she didn't want to experience again.

She stared at Amos. "You know it's not that simple. I might be an escort but I have a heart too. And I have more standards than probably all those groupies you meet." She shook her head. "I'm sorry, but I can't be with you, knowing you have another woman waiting for you at the end of tour."

Amos stopped a step away from her when he asked hoarsely, "Did you really believe a woman you don't know over a man who said he loves you?"

She drew in a breath, and then released it slowly, stopping herself from crossing her arms in a defensive gesture. Dear Lord. He was right. She didn't know Jasmine, had nothing on the other woman in which to base her trust. "She showed me your text message."

Amos' nostrils flared. "She's been stalking me for months, insisting we're meant to be together." His laugh had an edge. "We had a one-night stand and I thought that'd be the end of it. For Jasmine, it wasn't."

"Why didn't you tell me?" She croaked out.

"I didn't want to scare you." He dragged a hand over his face. "Besides, I'd imagined it was Jasmine's obsession that stopped me from wanting to form a serious relationship. Then I met you and I realized Jasmine had been a scapegoat, an excuse to avoid commitment."

"And now?"

"And now I realize nothing will stop be from claiming the woman I love more than anything... more than even my music."

Guilt pricked at her subconscious. He really did love her if he'd abandoned his first concert to be with her.

Harry turned to Amos and then back to Tiffany—no, Natalie—she'd truly always be Natalie now.

He sighed regretfully. "Well, I guess this means you two are getting back together again."

Natalie stood and took the final step to Amos, before throwing her arms around his neck. Her mouth met his in a kiss that rocked her to the core, and she only barely heard the cheers and clapping of the people witnessing the scene.

She pulled back with a big smile. She no longer cared if people heard about her profession and judged her. She wasn't ashamed, she was proud. Proud that a man like Amos loved her without bias. Proud that he loved her so much he didn't want to share her with any other man.

His eyes shone as he looked down at her and murmured, "I love you, Natalie. Don't ever doubt that again."

She nodded jerkily. There was no way she could speak past the huge lump in her throat. When Amos picked her up and carried her past the cheering crowd, she could barely see through her tears of joy.

She was finally where she was meant to be.

Epilogue

Natalie couldn't wipe the grin off her face as she watched Amos from one of the VIP front row seats. His voice filled her heart with more love than was surely possible, which seemed incredible, considering the song he now crooned had once made her cry.

My lover chose another
My heart might never recover
What did I do?
I only ever loved you...

She'd listened to that same song after Toby had professed his love for her, and then disappeared from her life. Now, the song filled her with giddy joy and anticipation, not pain.

She sang it along with him, blowing him a kiss when his gaze returned to find her yet again.

She'd missed a bullet when she and Toby hadn't gotten together, a bullet that would have bled her soul dry.

She'd blossomed under Amos' love and devotion.

"And now, I'd like to share a song I wrote for a very special lady... the love of my life." He walked across the stage and stood looking down at her. "Natalie, this one's for you."

Her lungs constricted, nervous energy and anticipation filling her as he sang about meeting a woman he wanted to marry. A kitten with claws and a heart of gold. She didn't realize she had tears streaming down her face—happy tears—until he finished his song, looked at her before he dropped on a knee and said huskily, "Natalie, will you marry me?"

She didn't recall leaving her seat and climbing onto the stage to cheers and whistles from the audience. She fell into his arms, laughing and babbling out, "Yes!" over and over.

He slid on a beautiful diamond engagement ring, kissed her one last time on the stage, and then nodded at his band mates. As they played a single from their latest album, Amos led her through the curtains and into the VIP room.

"There's just one thing I need to tell you before we marry," she said breathlessly.

His eyes darkened. "What is it?"

"I'd love to live in the country with you—at least, when you're not on tour—I wasn't being honest when I said I'd only ever live in the city."

His stare softened. "We can live in my Sydney house every second weekend if you like. Then we can go out for dinners and shopping trips, even manicures if that's your thing. And, of course, I'll have some rooms built onto the country house for your father and his carer... anything that is needed. And we can always escape to the mountain cabin when we need some privacy."

She smiled up at him, so happy her chest ached. "You know, I think I love you more every single day."

His eyes glowed as he murmured throatily, "And I plan on keeping it that way."

The End

Want more VIP Desire Agency stories by Mel Teshco...

Liberated

Also included in the VIP Desire Agency Boxset

Can two men conquer one woman's heart?

Eloise Chand isn't just any woman, she's also Savannah, stunning call girl. But it doesn't stop unprofessional thoughts about her favorite clients, Saxon and Julian. She knows she's in trouble. She doesn't want her career destroyed by personal attraction. She's a business woman first and foremost, and the Wolfe brothers aren't part of her career plan.

Adopted brothers, Saxon and Julian, share more than just their billion dollar real estate development business. But never in their wildest dreams did they expect to fall for the same call girl. She's a woman whose hot-blooded sexuality and independence stirs something deep in them both. That she's beyond willing to share the same bed with them is just a bonus they want to further explore.

But how do they permanently attain the one woman who just might be unattainable?

Chapter One of Liberated

Savannah took one last look at the middle-aged man snoring softly on the rumpled hotel bed, noting his taut face was now smoothed free of any stress, his mouth curled into a relaxed line.

Her own mouth tipped into a smile. She prided herself on keeping a client's often too demanding lifestyle at bay. She was every man's fantasy, a woman who could, for a short time at least, make her clients forget all about the harsher realities of life.

When her client woke tomorrow morning, he'd be returning to his courtroom dramas, at least until his next appointment with Savannah, his favorite call girl.

She gathered up her tip that consisted of a generous wad of hundred-dollar bills he'd left for her on the bedside table. Her client was a highly-paid judge and could well afford a night away from his stress-induced life.

Her smile died just a little at seeing the gold band on his finger. It was the one part of her profession she didn't like. Many of her clients were married men whose wives couldn't give them the sexual fantasies they obviously craved. Then again, it was probably a small price to pay for the judge's wife to turn a blind eye to any indiscretions.

Not that Savannah was in a position to judge anyone... least of all herself.

A lump formed in her throat when she recalled the poverty she and her family had lived in. That same poverty had forced her Nepalese parents to give her up at sixteen to an arranged marriage. It had been one less belly to feed, even though they'd had to borrow money for the dowry to give to the groom and his family.

She shuddered. Her older husband might have had the means to feed her, but she would have chosen an empty stomach any day over the sadistic violence he'd inflicted daily.

Yet she'd been the one who'd shamed and dishonored her family by running away to make a new life for herself in Australia. The tightness in her chest eased. She'd more than made it up to her family with the funds she sent them every month.

She tucked tonight's bonus into the apron's front pocket of her black-and-white maid's outfit, forcing the bleak memories of her past to the back of her mind where they belonged. Then, drawing in a steadying breath, she stepped past a mirrored wardrobe on the way to the front door.

She lifted a hand to pat her sleekly groomed, midnight-colored hair, noting her long-lashed, smudge-proof mascara, her crimson lipstick, and the rest of her made-up face that had sent her client into raptures was still all in place.

But it was her lackluster, dark-brown eyes that gave her pause. Her stare held not even a glint of emotion.

Damn. When had sex become so... lackluster?

It's never dull when you're with the Wolfe brothers.

A pity the brothers were also to blame for her present lack of passion. She swallowed convulsively. Acknowledging the truth didn't come easy. She'd worked hard at her profession, ensured she was at the top of her game. And now her favorite clients, Saxon and Julian Wolfe, threatened it all.

She squeezed her eyes closed and counted slowly to three. She wouldn't allow these stupid thoughts to destroy her composure. Except when she flicked open her lashes and her same hollow eyes stared back, the trickle of anxiety within threatened to turn into a flood.

She seldom felt anything but satisfaction at seeing a client writhe in ecstasy. But the emptiness growing inside was a serious risk to everything she'd worked so damn hard for.

She'd always enjoyed her work, but she realized now the more she saw Julian and Saxon, the more her emotions were becoming tangled with doubts. And the more she questioned what really made her happy.

She snapped off the overhead light and opened the front door, her thoughts still on the brothers. They always made sure they left her lipstick smudged and her hair tangled. And although dressing her up as a maid or a policewoman or any other fantasy figure wasn't their thing, sex with a beautiful woman most certainly was.

The adopted brothers might have different biological parents, but they shared more than just their billion-dollar real estate development business. They loved to fuck, and they most certainly loved to fuck her.

She shut the door behind her, then leaned her head against the door and closed her eyes again with a ragged sigh. Regardless of her concerns that she was breaking her one rule to never get close to a client, she wouldn't be quitting her addiction to the Wolfe brothers anytime soon.

An elevator dinged. She didn't hear anyone step into the corridor of the fourth floor, but her prickling skin and a rush of heat made her snap her eyes open. Her breath caught in her throat, her knees going weak at seeing the tall, powerful man leaning against the far wall.

"Saxon." She breathed out his name.

"Savannah," he said huskily in return, his heated, gun-metal stare sweeping over her and making her nipples peak even as she shivered with awareness.

Damn, did any man look better in a worn pair of jeans and a black T-shirt? She lifted her chin. "What are you doing here?"

It was almost involuntary to glance around the lighted corridor to see if he was alone. An unsettling feeling of disappointment sank in even as she shook her head and added, "You can't follow me. If Maisey hears about this, you'll be struck off my client list."

His being here was not okay. No man was allowed to intrude in business hours unless they were a client who'd paid for the privilege of her time. Maisey ran the VIP Desire Agency with an iron fist. She wouldn't put up with any transgressions, especially since she'd recently lost three of her best call girls to former clients.

Brandy, Scarlet, and Tiffany, otherwise known as Kate, Claire, and Natalie, had all found the loves of their lives. And Savannah was thrilled her best friends in the world had gotten out of an industry that could so easily corrode away self-worth.

But it didn't mean the Wolfe brothers could be the loves of her life. Yes, they took up way too much space in her head, but she'd learned to stand on her own two feet and make the most of a situation, and she refused to give another man the power to take away her freedom and independence.

Bad enough she was second-guessing everything about her career choice. She wouldn't hand them even more control.

Saxon stepped toward her, the dark brown of his hair burnished with glints of blond from his work in construction that often saw him outdoors. Even his stubble appeared blond against his sun-bronzed skin. "Maisey won't know unless you tell her, and we both know you won't do that."

Savannah bit back a sharp retort. There was no point lying, he knew better, just as Julian would have if he'd been here.

The unyielding set of Saxon's jaw was offset by the glint in his stare. "And you know why I'm here Savannah, but we won't beg, not even for you."

Of course they wouldn't. The brothers were notoriously proud, verging on arrogant. But they had every right to be. Their real estate development business hadn't become a huge success through luck and halfhearted work ethics. The brothers had worked their asses off and had earned every penny of their success.

"Where is Julian?" she asked weakly.

"He's working late again." His eyes glittered. "He didn't want to see you with another client."

Of course he didn't. Otherwise, she had no doubt it would have been Julian who'd be here trying to talk apparent sense into her. Julian with his eloquent speeches and persuasive charm. A master in the boardroom as well as the bedroom.

Not that Saxon lacked in any way. She shivered. He wasn't satisfied until she was satisfied. And although he was a man of few words, his blunt candor often put even more chinks in her armor.

She pressed the heel of her hand to her brow, suddenly hot and more than a bit anxious. The Wolfe brothers might be perfect for her body, but they weren't good for her mind. She'd never before questioned her career choice and now she felt like she was all but backed into a corner with no way out. "You shouldn't have come here either, Saxon."

His eyes darkened. "We mightn't beg, but we'll never give up on you, Savannah. You want us too, despite your denial."

Need and protest crawled through her in equal measure. Then he stilled in front of her, tall and forbidding. Her throat convulsed. Damn, he'd positively loom over her if it wasn't for her heels.

He braced his legs apart so he was closer to eye level, before he leaned forward, spreading his hands either side of the door behind her, his taut body effectively blocking any escape. And yet it wasn't fear that ratcheted up her heartbeat; it was adrenaline-fueled excitement and anticipation.

Her mouth dried and her belly churned with raw need. Yes, she went to bed with men for a living, but none of her clients took care of her like the Wolfe brothers. None of them made her feel like the Wolfe brothers did. Julian and Saxon looked after her as much as she looked after them. Her satisfaction was always their first objective.

Saxon dropped his head lower, trailing his lips across her lobe even as he murmured, "We want you, Savannah. Permanently. Tell me what we need to do to make you ours."

She squeezed her eyes closed, her breath hissing out even as his sandalwood scent filled her senses. She'd been at the receiving end of Saxon's body enough times now to know better than to fight their physical attraction. But she'd never give in, never lose her independence or allow any man to control her.

She'd escaped Nepal because of a man. Her breath hitched as the brutal memories again threatened to surface. She pushed them back. Her core beliefs hadn't changed. She wouldn't give away her rights to another man ever again.

Her lashes fluttered apart and she tilted back her head to look into the intensity of Saxon's stare. "I've already given you and Julian my answer," she whispered hoarsely. "I don't belong to anyone."

He shook his head, his expression intractable. "Whether you admit it or not, you do belong to us, Savannah. No one else will ever give you what we can." He cupped her face with a hand, and she forcibly restrained herself from leaning into his clasp. She'd always loved his rough, callused hands that revealed his hardworking lifestyle.

She shivered. Although Julian's hands were smoother, they were no less masterful.

"Tomorrow night, at least, you're ours." His words were a thick growl, making her bones turn to liquid and heat pool deep in her womb. "And don't imagine for a second we won't do everything in our power to change your mind."

If you would like to know when my next book is available, news, cover reveals and more, you can sign up for my newsletter: madmimi.com/signups/121695/join

Check out my website – http://www.melteshco.com/

You can also friend me on Facebook at https://www.facebook.com/mel.teshco

Or on my author Facebook page at https://www.facebook.com/MelTeshcoAuthor

And occasionally on Twitter at https://twitter.com/melteshco

Contact me: melteshco@yahoo.com.au

If you enjoy my books I'd be delighted if you would consider leaving a review. This will help other readers find my books.

About the Author

Mel Teshco loves to write scorching sci-fi and contemporary stories with an occasional paranormal thrown into the mix. Not easy with seven cats, two dogs and a fat black thoroughbred vying for attention, especially when Mel's also busily stuffing around on Facebook. With only one daughter now living at home to feed two minute noodles, she still shakes her head at how she managed to write with three daughters and three stepchildren living under the same roof. Not to mention Mr. Semi-Patient (the one and same husband hoping for early retirement...he's been waiting a few years now.) Clearly anything is possible, even in the real world.

The VIP Desire Agency: series order
Lady in Red (book 1)
High Class (book 2)
Exclusive (book 3)
Liberated (book 4)
Uninhibited (book 5)
The VIP Desire Agency Boxed Set (all 5 books in the series)
The Virgin Hunt Games volume 1
The Virgin Hunt Games volume 2
The Virgin Hunt Games volume 3
Coming soon
The Virgin Hunt Games volumes 4-6
Alien Hunger: series order
Galactic Burn (book 1)
Galactic Inferno (book 2)
Galactic Flame (book 3)
Coming soon
Galactic Blaze (book 4)
Nightmix: series order:
Lusting the Enemy (book 1)
Abducting the Princess (book 2)
Seducing the Huntress (book 3)
Dragons of Riddich: series order:
Kadin (free prequel - book 1)
Asher (book 2)
Baron (book 3)
Dahlia (book 4)
Wyatt (book 5)
Valor (book 6)
The Queen (book 7)
Winged & Dangerous: series order
Stone Cold Lover (book 1)

Ice Cold Lover (book 2)
Red Hot Lover (book 3)
Winged & Dangerous Box Set (all 3 books in the series)
Box sets with authors Christina Phillips & Cathleen Ross
Taken by the Sheikh
Taken by the Billionaire
Taken by the Desert Sheikh
Resisting the Firefighter
Dirty Sexy Space continuity with authors Shona Husk and Denise Rossetti:
Yours to Uncover (book 1)
Mine to Serve (book 6)
Ours to Share (book 8)
Standalone longer length titles: (50k-100k)
Mutant Unveiled
Shadow Hunter
Highest Bid
As I Am
Existence
Standalone novellas and short stories: (15k-35K)
Identity Shift
Moon Thrall
Blood Chance
Carnal Moon
Stripped
Clarissa
Camilla
Selena's Bodyguard (also part of the Christmas Assortment Box)
Anthologies:
Down and Dusty: The Complete Collection
The Christmas Assortment Box
Secret Confessions: Sydney Housewives

Coming soon from December 2021: (Pre-order)
The Sheikh's Runaway Bride
The Sheikh's Captive Lover

Don't miss out!

Visit the website below and you can sign up to receive emails whenever Mel Teshco publishes a new book. There's no charge and no obligation.

https://books2read.com/r/B-A-ZFLB-LSZRB

BOOKS2READ

Connecting independent readers to independent writers.

www.ingramcontent.com/pod-product-compliance
Ingram Content Group UK Ltd.
Pitfield, Milton Keynes, MK11 3LW, UK
UKHW041823200726
13854UKWH00002BA/516

9 798201 010898